Lights of The Row

Stephen Rowley

Pyxis Editions

Published by Pyxis Editions
77 Kingston Road, Taunton, United Kingdom
info@pyxiseditions.co.uk

ISBN: 978-0-9567152-1-0

Printed and bound by CPI Group (UK) Ltd, Croydon, CR0 4YY

Contents

The Real McCoy 1

Hugh McDonnell is Saved 19

Shit 33

Dumb Show 45

Ironies 59

The Fight 77

Initiation 87

Plunder 111

The Scarf 121

The Match 137

Touched 149

Gentle into that Good Night 167

Toilet Blues 181

"Two-thirds of thy gentleness be shown to women and those who creep on the floor (little children) and to poets, and be not violent to the common people ..."

from *The Maxims of the Fianna*

The Real McCoy

Number 21 Kensington Street belonged to Archibald Jackson. It was halfway down the left-hand side looking across from Mosie Hunter's public house. In all the streets around Sandy Row, there was not one house that remotely resembled number 21 Kensington Street. The doors of many houses were painted surprising—even eccentric—colours which in a way lifted them out of the grey-brick monochrome; but not one aspired to the originality of number 21. Other brightly coloured houses in the Row existed but they were painted in a statement of uniform loudness and, although eye-catching, their overall conformity to the effort of individualisation served to underline the logic of the amorphous and achromatic whole they were unmistakably part of. Number 21 escaped the logic of the street.

Any visitor from outside the Row who was obliged to leave his car to the curiosity of the local children in order to carry out his business in Shaftesbury Square, could not help but stare in amazement and condescending horror at the exterior of Archibald's house. The mixtures of red and yellow brickwork, patched with blue, green and orange tiles scattered haphazardly across the façade, made a violent attack upon the optical nerves. Purple cement diamonds were set in bas-relief and protruded assertively from their backgrounds, while the windows were full of dark-green fleshy plants with vivid red flowers that held themselves back artificially and accentuated the illusion of depth. The façade of the entire house was exactly the same dimensions as the others in the street, and although it was squeezed in between the Crawtons and the Rileys, Archibald had undoubtedly succeeded in making it stand out from the rest through its sheer visual eccentricity. It looked bigger than it actually was. The onlooker was drawn into it, pulled into the rich orgy of colour and inimitable shapes like a child looking incredulously into a box of brightly-wrapped sweets.

The interior of Archibald's house—to which one gained access by stepping over a ridge of turquoise tiles—was equally as idiosyncratic as the exterior. On entering the tiny three-by-four kitchen-come-parlour with its oversized open-range fire, one was assailed by a barrage of sound. Archibald possessed eighty-seven clocks. All shapes and sizes, all sorts of ticks and chimes and clangs, from all over the world. About two-thirds of them kept more or less the same time, but it was the other thirty-or-so renegades that, by going off at irregular and totally unexpected intervals, really gave the room its notes of eccentricity.

Archibald's open fireplace was the only one left in the street—a fact which on its own would have made him a singular character since everyone else had long ago installed the Electricity Board's log or coal-effect which beamed out clinically and cleanly from the centre of its wooden surrounds. But downstairs room had no settee or armchair: instead, projecting from the sides of the grate were hard, low seats covered with foam. Two hard-backed chairs made the area into a cosy, if not comfortable, semi-circle crouched in worship of the fire. That was all the room possessed in terms of furniture. Plus the clocks. Clocks ticking, pendules swinging, little brass balls in dome-shaped German clocks rotating, Swiss cuckoos popping in and out, and little red soldiers hammering and marching out through one door and in through another, incessantly.

Archibald sat day after day amidst this whirligig of sound. Being perpetually surrounded by an anarchy of ticks, time meant both everything and nothing to him. He knew his clocks. Even the rebellious thirty-or-so that refused to march in time with the others, he knew by heart. He knew which cuckoo was going to thrust itself out next; which leaden ball had to be pulled up at a certain time; which seven-day clock was due to run out. It was quite a feat remembering when to wind them up as they did not all work on a 24-hour basis, and the 'cranks' as he called them, more or less kept to their own time. He was particularly proud of his cranks. Some had pieces broken and periodically needed 'doctored'. He would spend many of his spare moments performing the surgery with meticulous concern, fiddling with their 'innards' until he patiently got them to tick again. He had a watch on a chain as old as himself. His father had bought it when he was born and had given it to him on his twenty-first birthday. 'Archibald Congal Jackson' (no one knew where the middle name came from) was inscribed with a flourish on the back. He had thought of getting rid of it on many occasions, but somehow it stuck with him, even through the wars. But it too was a crank and kept to its own time. He was forever taking it apart, cleaning it and putting it back together again. He felt curiously restored after one of these operations.

Archibald was happiest when, in the presence of his usual midday visitor, his 'old faithfuls' would suddenly strike up more or less simultaneously, forcing his interlocutor into a resentful, but nevertheless respectful, silence. Archibald would go into a trance as they began to hammer the first of the midday strokes: chiming, striking, soldiers, cuckoos and whirling balls contributing to the infernal din, the clamour of clang and clatter lasting not twelve but maybe twenty billowing blows and echoes, from the first bong of the grandfather clock to the last twitter of the cuckoo-crying noon.

Mr McDonnell from number 45 was one of Archibald's few visitors who actually enjoyed being interrupted by a rogue clock. On a Saturday morning, when his wife left him to potter about the house while she did the weekly shopping down Sandy Row, he would often decide to dander along to number 21 just to be included in the weekend bustle which seemed to be intensified in Archibald's house by the clocks. It really felt like 'panic stations' as they were fond of describing it—both men having been in the armed forces. Mr McDonnell had seventeen years of broken service in the Air Force and had been made a corporal several times. He was well respected in the street—in what might be described as a legitimate way, as he was the head of a family which saved money and seemed to be going somewhere, whilst at the same time keeping its feet firmly rooted in the street. Archibald's respect was of a different nature. It was common knowledge that he had fought—both at home and abroad—and everyone was grateful for this. He had been a private all his life—had refused to be anything else—and had served faithfully and unquestionably: when told to polish some officer's brass, he had done so with the same conviction and gusto with which he had charged when told to run at the enemy. And he had run like a mad dog, crying "Ya bastards!" And he had returned, albeit in pieces, from the edge of death. He had returned with a glass eye, and a bullet in him somewhere. He had fought two wars in France, Italy and Germany. It was from these countries that he had brought back his many souvenirs, the clocks. And brass shell and bullet cases he used to decorate his mantelpiece; along with a bullet somewhere in his body; and, most strikingly of all, the glass ball in his left eye socket which was blue-irised and stood out with the dim reflection of his brasses, clocks and bullet cases.

People seemed to differentiate between Archibald the war veteran, and Archibald the crackpot who decorated the exterior of his poky house so unorthodoxly; who possessed exotic and succulent plastic plants; who had a room full of clocks; and who had constructed a roof garden on top of his scullery (to which one gained access via the toilet). This Archibald was reckoned to be a 'headcase'. He was laughable, but not to his face, for then the two Archibalds came together and it was easy to imagine this mad dog running at you with a bayonet, if his blood was up.

Of course people gossiped, and he enjoyed giving them a lot to go on about. In particular, he was the proud father of two girls who made quite a stir, even beyond the neighbourhood. His wife, Ma Jackson, was a chain-smoker who hadn't very much to say for herself and said it with admirable discretion. As soon as one Woodbine was on the point of extinguishing itself, she would puff on another, thus maintaining an unending fire on her fingertips and a blue haze which hid her face. Her eyes were already behind thick concentric-ringed lenses which reduced them to two, black, piercing points. She never inhaled the smoke, but held it in the mouth and then snorted it down the nostrils like a dragon. Ma had vertical wrinkles on her lips which made her mouth look stitched around the dangling weed. She would just sit and puff; make the tea and puff; poke the fire and puff; never giving anyone any offence, and never getting offended. But the girls had none of their mother's self-effacement. Without a doubt they were made of their father's metal, for they possessed more than a trace of his singularity of character.

The street might sooner or later have come to accept Archibald's house sticking out like a spangled barber's pole from the prevailing drabness and uniformity; they might have come to accept his wild plants, his roof-garden, and even—in the end—his bloody clocks: but the two girls would never permit the Jackson household to be assimilated by the neighbours. They bore the indelible stamp of their father's fabrication which flaunted originality and eccentricity and flung any possibility of quiet acceptance by the street right back in its face. They would be different, no matter what.

Germaine was twenty-one, and Catherine (Cate for short) was nineteen. They were both sensually attractive girls, swarthy-complexioned, with coal-black hair and large brown eyes. There was something about them which struck the onlooker as being African. True, the hair was a bit frizzy, but it was more the way they carried themselves—with their backsides pointed curiously upward and their backs curved—or the way they sprawled on a chair with a certain vulnerable, sensuous negligence, that made one think of paintings of the southern hemisphere. It was for them that Archibald had built the roof garden. In spite of their tanned complexion, they had never been to the lands of the sun-soaked brochures. The roof garden enabled them to take full advantage of Belfast's limited annual sun allowance in order to deepen their swarthiness. Archibald had cemented an area of about six square yards on top of his scullery and toilet, and surrounded this with a two-foot wall which he suggested was to protect the girls from the dirty eyes of the neighbours, but which was really to protect them from the wind which whistled between the backs of the houses.

He had brought many exotic plastic plants up to the roof, and even a few real ones which, peculiarly enough, looked surprisingly artificial by comparison. He had found space for two deckchairs, and a small coffee table. The girls would usually lie in the deckchairs with their legs spilling over the convenient wall. It had never been their desire to be preserved from being gobbled up by the greedy eyes of the local males or the envious eyes of their wives. Life would have been far too dull. Any Saturday morning, when the air was not too cutting and the sun only moderately obscured by clouds, one could look out the back window of any of the houses in the row and perceive Germaine or Catherine lying there, almost naked offerings to the reluctant and embarrassed sun, and one could get a whiff—if the wind struck up (as it usually did)—of the heady odour of holidays carried in the oily waft of Ambre Solaire.

It would be true to say that when Archibald had finished the construction of the roof garden, it had created a sensation. Even the papers got to hear about it. A man from *The Telegraph* came round to snap Germaine and Catherine in all their glory, and a photograph duly appeared in one of the inside pages of that illustrious guide to Belfast life. Of course, most readers had never heard of Kensington Street or where it might be found, but the description of the size of the house left them in no doubt as to why the roof garden was an oddity. The girls got a write-up that more than pleased old Archibald. The photographer complimented himself on having discovered—right there in Belfast, not far from Sandy Row of all places—'two long-legged beauties fit to adorn any Californian beach.'

Nevertheless, the girls had gained a bit of a reputation in the area. They had had many boyfriends, and were known to be looking for husbands, although it was also acknowledged that their ambitions lay far beyond Kensington Street. They dressed in a shocking manner, usually in outrageous colours, flying a challenge to everyone and a provocation to easily excitable males. But it was not so much the colour of their dress which so shocked the neighbourhood; rather it was the fact that there was so little of the material itself. Catherine in particular had shed her bra long before anyone had ever heard of feminism, and, since she was quite luxuriously built in that area, the absence never failed to be conspicuous. They were often referred to as 'shameless hussies' in the run-of-the-mill gossip which was the manna of the street. Mrs McDonnell, despite the fact that her husband was a friend of Archibald's, once gave her eldest son a beating when she found him on the corner after dark with one of the girls: "Don't let me catch you with that hussy again!" she threatened him, and despite the fact that he was seventeen and earning a living, she clouted him fiercely across the back of the head.

But the girls had at present, very regular boyfriends who were more than eligible. Germaine was 'going with' a law student who was absolutely mad about her. He was from a good family from up the Malone Road and had already proposed to the girl. She procrastinated in the full knowledge—which in her case was instinctive—that he would press her all the harder. Her fish was well hooked. Catherine, on the other hand, was not on marital terms with her boyfriend, but was certainly using him to good effect. He worked for Ulster Television, and had introduced her to many of his influential friends. The latter, struck by her beauty (perhaps her lack of bra too), were proving to be valuable contacts. The photograph of her almost entirely unclad swarthiness appeared in papers and magazines, and she was even getting offers of parts in films as an 'extra'. There was little doubt in her mind that she was already part-way down the road to Hollywood.

Archibald was proud of his girls. They would make it, indeed they already had in the most important ways. As for rumours and reputations, he had no time for them. When he thought of the other people in the street he simply shrugged them off as jealous, spat into the hot grate and was cheered by his sizzling saliva. What did he care about other people's opinions? Sure, weren't his girls good to him and Ma? Didn't they bring him nice presents? Just lately he had received a somewhat ordinary-looking, though obviously expensive, wooden clock from Germaine's law student who was already behaving like a decent son-in-law. Yes, he could be proud of them; just as they were proud of him, and not at all inhibited about bringing their wealthy suitors into the poky little downstairs room of number 21. It even became a kind of test. One suspected that the girls enjoyed watching the wriggling of uncomfortable would-be suitors unable to come to terms with the house and its environment. From these refined callers Archibald also obtained a perverse sort of pleasure by offering them tea in a chipped mug, or 'Snake's Blood' straight from the bottle. "If a man can't drink from a bat'le he's gat no ballocks an' he's no son-in-law for me!" he would swankily say, and then spit-sizzle into the grate.

During one of their regular Saturday morning meetings, Archibald and Mr McDonnell sat quietly chatting—or 'gabblin" as Mrs McDonnell would later remind her husband—about Hitler's mistake in taking on the Russians; the exploits of the Bismarck; and the joke of the Maginot Line. Archibald sat in an upright position, one foot on the hearth-fender and the other on the rung of his chair. Ma Jackson sat puffing in the scullery, as Archibald always liked to be alone with his company. Catherine was still in bed and Germaine out shopping with her Andrew. It was in the middle of a discussion on the length of the Bismarck's guns that the familiar noise of a car engine was heard to approach from the bottom of the street. Archibald's hearing was still sharp and he moved his head to one side, closing his real eye in an attempt to focus his attention, leaving the other eye staring vacantly as if he had just been struck dumb. Mr McDonnell could distinguish nothing beyond the noise of the clocks, until the roar of the engine was right outside the door. Andrew's red sports car always created a sensation in the street. Just at the sound of it people came inquisitively to their windows to draw back the curtains. Germaine stepped out, slammed the door, and was heard to say something about "seven-thirty".

"Bet ya she's loaded wi' things!" and Archibald tapped his thigh and winked his eye at his guest whose attention was unfortunately taken by the eye which did not close, but who laughed knowingly all the same. Germaine's stilettos clicked on the turquoise tiles, and when she pushed open the door her hands were full of parcels. Her father beamed.

"An' hi's our lawyer today then?" he asked maliciously.

"Nat bad … says he'll come in tanight—no time nigh." The girl immediately passed through the kitchen to the scullery to greet her mother. She popped her head out again to say "Hello," to Mr McDonnell who nodded appreciatively. Archibald leaned over to his friend and whispered:

"He's swallowed it hook, line an' sinker!" and sniffed delightedly before clearing his throat.

"Gonna be a lawyer … *ed-u-ca-ted*, ya know?" and here he paused, as if to let the full meaning of the word sink in.

"Edyacated! That's a good 'un! More friggin' sense in one o' them cuckoos!" He nodded towards one of the clocks on the wall, slapped his thigh again, and then roared with laughter. Mr McDonnell laughed with him, and just then—as if in total agreement—a cuckoo popped out and announced that it was a quarter-past or a quarter-to something.

"Aye, she's gat 'im right where sh' wants 'im, ya know? No doubt about it."

"She'll do all right for herself, will Germaine," confirmed Mr McDonnell authoritatively.

Archibald became silent. He looked pensively at the prepared-yet-unlit fire in the dark grate. The weather was not cold. His guest became aware of the clocks again, their heavy ticking seemed to hang in the air like someone's breath. Archibald suddenly looked up, his real eye round and large like his glass one, making him look wildly insane.

"Mind you … don't think 'e doesn't know what 'e's doin' … 'e knows what 'e's gettin' in our Germaine, all right. Friggin' good bargain, if ya ask me. She'll nat let 'im down … an' she's nat one o' them high faluters who don't know their arses from their elbows an' 'd run a mile if they ever seen a dick … she'll give 'im what 'e wants 'n plenty of it."

"Aye, she's a well-built girl like, ya know," said Mr McDonnell, looking into Archibald's sightless eye which was easier to watch, as the other one moved frantically from side to side.

"Aye," Archibald acquiesced, "bastardin' real thing, she is!" Silence again as the clocks motioned. Archibald stretched forward and put a light to the ready fire.

Germaine brought two mugs of tea into the room, and sat them on the mantelpiece above the newly-born fire which was growing rapidly. "Ma says 'ere's yar tea," and as she turned to walk back, Archibald patted her lightly on the bottom. Germaine turned on him venomously: "Don't do that da!" and walked out angrily. She climbed up on to the roof.

"'E'll nat regret it," said Archibald, staring at the shiny black coal which was just starting to catch. Mr McDonnell felt somewhat uneasy because of what had just happened and reached for his tea which he quickly began to gulp down. It was lukewarm—Ma had obviously poured it before sitting down with another Woodbine. Mr McDonnell decided to leave at the earliest opportunity, but he was held by the fire beginning to dance in the grate.

Archibald was not ready yet to let him go as he did not think his guest had been sufficiently impressed as to the suitability of the forthcoming marriage. He stood up, mug in hand, and declared that his guest could not leave before seeing the magnificent roses that were just beginning to come into colour in his roof-garden. Consequently, both men began moving towards the scullery, leaving the room which now seemed to Mr McDonnell to be overheated.

They went through the curtain and passed the steep, narrow staircase which led to the two upstairs rooms, into the tiny scullery which was momentarily empty as Ma had gone upstairs to make the bed. The scullery was dark and dingy, and the yellow-stained sink was piled high with dishes which Ma was hoping one of the girls would wash. Mr McDonnell almost had his eye poked out by the handle of an egg-flip which protruded from a frying pan of hardened fat hanging from the side of the grill above the cooker. This was not Archibald's domain and he walked through it unflinchingly as if it were a foreign land full of unfriendly natives.

They went through a door into a small yard which harboured the toilet. Archibald had put a ladder against the latter edifice, and the two men began to mount, Mr McDonnell first, mugs in hand. As he reached the top of the ladder, Mr McDonnell was suddenly confronted with Germaine's sprawling legs, naked to the thigh, as she had drawn her muslin skirt to her lap in an attempt to encourage the sun's fleeting caress. The sight had the effect Archibald desired, and the old man grinned with satisfaction as Mr McDonnell's foot searched desperately for the rung of the ladder. His guest was quick to recover himself and managed to climb somewhat clumsily on to the roof of the scullery where he was met by the radiant smile of the reclining figure, eager to put him at ease after his involuntary indiscretion. But the smile in turn made him more uneasy, for something struck him as being terrifyingly naked and equine in the brazen exposure of all those strong, white and sturdily gleaming teeth set off against the girl's swarthy skin. Mr McDonnell hastily turned his attention to the flowers.

"That's a beauty!" he exclaimed, squirming his way past the stem of the girl's long and succulent body, and pointing to a dark-blue iris-shaped plant which turned out to be a fake. Immediately aware of his mistake, he clutched on to some pinks which could not possibly be imitation. But they were.

Archibald came to the rescue by pointing out the half-opened buds of the scarlet roses hiding just behind his daughter's head which was now inclined backwards in communication with the sun which had just decided to show its face again. Mr McDonnell noticed, despite his confusion, that Germaine had slipped the straps of her garment off her shoulders.

"But they're not real, are they?" he cried with sincere disbelief. And it was true that the intensely scarlet, vivid beauty of the half-opened buds seemed almost surreal. Theirs was such a deep, yet sensitive beauty, one as strong and fleeting as the sun itself, that they looked false juxtaposed as they were with the shiny, superficial colours of the other flowers.

"Aye, they're the real thing alright. Nathin' can bate a real flar, ya know," said Archibald, but his attention was fixed on the almost fully-opened body of the reclining figure whose heavy limbs they gingerly had to circumnavigate for fear of falling back into the yard.

The row of houses on Archibald's side of Kensington Street were back-to-back with a row of the same from Wesley Street, with not so much as a gunnel to separate them. This quite naturally gave rise to a lot of promiscuity as, from the window of one back bedroom, one could see into the back bedrooms of about a dozen houses opposite. Curiosity was only rarely obstructed by curtains or window blinds which were kept for windows at the front, giving on to the street. Mr McDonnell looked over the tops of the plastic flowers, and searched for something of interest in the houses opposite. He gazed up the row to the far end which finished in the blank wall of Thompson's bakery. Near the top was a gap caused by the advent of Stroud Street cutting in from Sandy Row. The wall of Mrs Gillin's house, immediately after the gap, was higher than the others and topped with a jagged layer of broken beer bottles that flashed green and brown in the sunshine. Much of the back guttering of the houses was broken, as could be seen from the vertical lines of moss which ran down from the slated roofs to the inside yards. Many of the windows were cracked or had bits missing and were permanently blocked by pieces of cardboard or pasted newspaper. The slate roofs also caught the sunlight and tossed it on to the grey walls. In the yard touching the Jacksons, Mr McDonnell could see an upturned dustbin with rubbish spewing out of it. The toilet was full of bottles and tin cans which slobbered over into the yard. Mr McDonnell felt that it was time to go.

He drained his mug and began clambering down the ladder, pausing momentarily to take a helpless last look at the girl's body which spilled over the deckchair like an over-ripe fruit. He said "Cheerio!" to Germaine, who answered with another unrestrained exposure of her equine teeth. Archibald followed him down.

They manoeuvred their way through the drab little scullery, and he bade farewell to the cloud of smoke which had returned to the stool and could be identified as Ma Jackson.

"Thanks for the tea," he ventured towards the haze which seemed to nod forward. Catherine was beginning to stir upstairs and this conveyed a sense of urgency to Mr McDonnell's departure. He moved back into the room where the fire was now aglow and throwing out heat which he found stifling. He moved to the door giving on to the street and turned to say goodbye to his host. Archibald nodded to him in recognition. Though he was eager to find relief from the heat by crossing the doorstep, he paused for a moment. Then he turned again to Archibald and began a sentence, thoughtfully …

"Aye, she's the …" but no sooner had he begun, than the clocks struck up midday. The two grandfathers began thundering in sequence; cuckoos popped in and out (and there was a distinct 'cuckoo-koo-koo'); doors opened and closed as soldiers marched in with hammers to ching bells; clocks chimed and knocked and the small room rocked in the concurrent waves of sound which clashed in the cacophony.

When it had almost died down, Mr McDonnell looked up at Archibald who was standing in obvious ecstasy, with his mouth and one eye wide open. Then he too came to a standstill, the last vibrations of his body mingling with the resonant waves, straightening into silence. He gazed expectantly at his departing guest.

"… the real McCoy!" the latter said, opening the door and at last stepping relievedly over the turquoise tiles and into the reassuring sounds of Saturday lunchtime.

Hugh McDonnell
is Saved

The Firbags were a family of eleven—nine healthy and rowdy children, ranging from the newly-born Edith to the eldest Sammy, just turned thirteen. They lived in number 41 Kensington Street, midway between Mrs Gillins and Cinnamon's butcher shop. The father, Tommy, had his own horse and cart and was a rag-and-bone man most of the time, although he seemed to have many occupations. Tommy was a notorious fighter and gambler. His house was directly opposite the bookmakers and both edifices were like communicating vessels that spilled into one another with noise, smoke and endless activity. In his younger days, Tommy had carried a hatchet hung inside his long overcoat. But time had settled upon him a quiet middle age and a lazy appetite for financial gain. He rode around most of the time looking for discarded clothes or rusty washing machines, but kept an eye open for the bric-a-brac of the past for which he had an increasing market in a well-situated shop at the top of Sandy Row.

Tommy supervised the activities of his five sons: Sammy and Charlie helped daily on the cart; Frankie chopped, bundled and sold sticks; Tommy Junior and the youngest, Robbie, were farmed out to work for an uncle who had no offspring of his own. Tommy was usually polite and friendly until he had drunk himself into a crass and malevolent oblivion. But despite his own numerous weaknesses, he was happy in the thought that he looked after the children's future, as well as their religious education which he fostered by sending them to Sunday school and to the Monday Night Mission.

Every Monday evening, six of the Firbags were bundled out to the Emmanuel Mission Hall, a solid stone-built edifice in Wellwood Street. As they spilled out through the door of number 41, the house seemed to deflate and push out a sigh of relief, leaving the mother happily to her infants, in the absence of older children and husband, the latter preferring the sanctuary of Mosie Hunter's tabernacle.

Sammy, Charlie, Frankie, Joy, Sadie and Tommy Junior jostled with other children as they shoved their way through the heavy wooden doors of the Emmanuel Mission Hall. An unusually clear April evening found all the children in very high spirits. They were cheering and choking, spitting, kicking and yelping Indian noises, when suddenly an almighty "Shooo!" met them from the inside of the Hall. The 'shooo', the children knew, was from Mr Hands, a very clean and lean lay preacher who had the proud good fortune to be buying a small house at the top of the Donegall Road. The aptly named Mr Hands was almost middle class. He always wore a suit; was clean-shaven with impeccably-groomed hair; and impressed the children by the exceptional whiteness of his hands which radiated a light of their own and dazzled the children by the blanche purity of the fingernails and the band of gold which reflected the electric light. The fingernails established some mystical, partly-understood equation in the children's minds between whiteness and all the things they would probably never have. Mr Hands' skin was certainly next to godliness—if not directly of the same material— and the children revered him more than any of the other preachers they were forced into contact with. His 'shooo' therefore brought immediate calm to the festivities, and they filed timidly into his beckoning arms which ushered them to the hard wooden benches in front of the pulpit.

With the heavy doors closed, the room they sat in seemed to enclose a sort of warm, soothing pinkishness which bathed the brown oak beams of the ceiling in an unnatural softness. The arch of the ceiling was so far above them that it might have been the floor of heaven itself. Here they had space and distance and silence, and perhaps because of the unfamiliarity of these things, the children huddled together on the front benches leaving those at the back empty to magnify the space.

Hugh McDonnell was ten years old, and lived two doors from the Firbags in number 45 Kensington Street. He was good friends with the second eldest of the Firbag boys, but thought, in a rather superior way, that the whole clan could have washed more frequently. He always attended the Monday Night Mission, but never sat with the Firbags because their behaviour often embarrassed him. Hugh had almost been won over to Mr Hands. Tonight, he sat behind the eldest Firbag girl, Joy, but was only aware of the sweet odour of Mr Hands' aftershave lotion which reached out to him persuasively to be attentive.

Mr Hands delivered the first, short prayer of some three or four sentences in complete silence. When it was time to rise for the first song, his helper—Jimmy Philpott—a balding, middle-aged man with a squeezed-up body which made him appear to the children as an evil gnome newly converted to the service of the Lord, moved to the front of the Hall and began turning over the giant pages of the book hanging from the wooden railing at the front of the wide pulpit. He stopped at the song 'Running Over'; turned to his young audience with small, malicious eyes, and began to lead them into song on the piano. It was a welcome release from the silence, and the children showed their appreciation by immediately roaring up into lusty voice:

> *Running over, running over*
> *My cup's full and running over*
> *Since the Lord saved me*
> *I'm as happy as can be*
> *My cup's full and running over.*

Most of the public sang light-heartedly in tune; a few deliberately did the opposite; one or two just squawked anything that came into their heads; whilst Sammy Firbag substituted his own words which in no way coincided with the rhythms of the hymn: "Kick the Pope and No Surrender!/Bash his balls against a fender. We'll go on wi' No Surrender!/Bash 'em all th' harder." He was careful to keep his voice low when the other song did not cover him. The effect he was having on those close to him made him go on longer than he would normally have deemed safe. They heard his words but crashed on enthusiastically with 'Running Over', carrying out the gestures demanded by the song. Mr Philpott, on reaching the final note, stopped abruptly and squinted intensely at the children who finished at different intervals. Their mirth had alerted him to something going on, but he had missed it this time.

The room settled into an uneasy silence, out of which the quietly controlled voice of Mr Hands rose to caress them. "Well, now that we've all warmed up, I'm going to talk to you about a little friend of mine called Billy. Now Billy was about your age when he first met the Lord Jesus but before meeting the Lord Jesus, Billy was far from being a good boy ..."

One of the Firbags let off, and this triggered a bout of embarrassed childish snickering. Hugh McDonnell reddened and looked down at his feet. Mr Philpott leered murderously at Sammy Firbag who shook his head in innocent protest. Mr Hands continued with more firmness in his voice.

"No, Billy wasn't a nice boy at all. He used to call others names, and bit them for no reason ... he would even tell lies about them. He disobeyed his parents. But more than that boys and girls," here he paused to look around him, "Billy used to *steal.*" Mr Hands emphasised this word by staring disbelievingly into the air. The children followed his gaze expectantly.

"Yes, boys and girls … he used to steal. He used to run past the grocer's shop and lift fruit—apples or bananas—or go into the sweet shop and stuff all he could into his pockets when the shopkeeper wasn't looking. Billy would steal from anybody …" Mr Hands paused dramatically a second time to scrutinise the upheld faces of the children. "One day, it happened that Billy needed sixpence to go to the pictures …"

During this brief interval, Charlie Firbag turned knowingly to his elder brother to say, "We cud a gat 'im in for nathin'!" but their mirth was restrained by Mr Philpott's wicked stare.

"Do you know what he did, this little Billy? He went to his mother's purse and took from it a shiny silver sixpence. Yes, boys and girls, that's what he did! He took the money from his own mother!" Again there was a pause and a verification that the audience had taken in the enormity of the offence.

"But it wasn't time to go to the pictures yet, so what did he do? He crept sneakily upstairs and hid the money under one of the floorboards, which was his usual place for putting things he had to conceal from the light of day. Billy thought that no one could see him; that no one could find him out. He felt safe because he was persuaded that no one would ever discover his black little secret. But he was wrong boys and girls, for you know what he forgot?" This pause made all the children feel as if they were being individually questioned. Hugh McDonnell searched for an answer on the pale walls of the Hall which seemed to move strangely closer to him. But Mr Hands was not looking for an answer. He went on:

"He forgot of course that *God* could see him—that *God* was finding him out. God can see everything we do; He is with us everywhere we go. We can't hide anything from God, you know. Even the blackest of your secrets you will find written in a book in the clearest of handwriting. And what happened to Billy? He heard his mother come in downstairs, and when she opened her purse and saw that the sixpence was gone, she sat down and cried." The sorrow of Billy's mother touched even the most boisterous amongst the children and they sat in total silence, spellbound. Mr Hands went on:

"But Billy was lucky, yes sir!, because at that moment God spoke to his heart and opened up his love for his mother. God spoke to him and told him to put the money back. He said: 'Let the Lord Jesus, who died on Calvary for your sins, let him come into your heart. Put the money back Billy.' And Billy listened to the words of God, and did what God told him—he put the money back!"

Mr Hands' voice was full of awe and wonder born of the miracle he had just formulated. He smiled and looked gratefully at the thick walls around him. The children fixed on to his radiant face and saw it in the full flush of the dying sun which was streaming through a coloured half-moon window above the door. Mr Hands began again:

"His mother took Billy in her arms and kissed him and ever since that day, I can tell you, Billy has been a far happier boy. When he wants something, he no longer steals it; he asks or runs errands or does wee jobs in order to earn it. Billy has learned the meaning of God's words and he has the wealth of the Lord Jesus in his heart. Now children, are you going to be like Billy? Are you going to let the Lord Jesus into *your* heart? Don't pretend that you do not hear God speaking to you, calling to you to come forward. And there's no good putting it off until tomorrow—we all have that laziness which is just an easy way out—because tomorrow might just be too late: when you think some day that you are about ready for God, He might just not be ready for you. So why not now, boys and girls? Why not today? Let the Lord Jesus come into your heart tonight."

Many people did not like Mr Hands. The holy whiteness which seemed to shine through his flesh kept people at a distance. A holy light which repelled others by its mystic intensity and self-righteousness. But the same white light was this evening beaming out to the children and washing them in the milk of human kindness and godly generosity. At the height of his appeal, Mr Hands opened up like a white camellia and gathered them in the fragrance of his goodness. The children were anointed; they were touched. Hugh McDonnell felt his body tingle and sway and he turned his head upwards to the wide arch of the ceiling to search for the eyes of the Unknown, to listen for the bleating of the white lamb of Jesus.

"Now children, let us pray," said the holy man.

Mr Hands led them in prayer. Their voices were in unison, the words blessed with the wonder of a world beyond. When he had finished—before the enchantment was lost—he carried them through more songs. Mr Philpott took to the piano again and the children blasted their way through 'Climb, Climb Up Sunshine Mountain', 'Deep and Wide', and 'Jesus Loves the Little Children'. It was a glorious cacophony which thoroughly exhausted them all. When the last notes of the piano petered out, the room spread itself and plopped weightily down on to the benches. Wild humours were left breathless. Outside, the world was dark-turning, and a final bloodshot ray slanted through the stained-glass cross at the end of the Hall.

Mr Hands raised his long arms like white-tipped antennae: "Now, just before we break up for this evening, it is time for the distribution of tonight's prizes." The children promptly sat erect on the edge of their seats with arms folded and elbows trying to point towards the pulpit, some of them saying, "Me sir! Me sir!" as if chanting. Mr Hands opened a green velvet cloth, heavy with treasures. He spread it before him. There were rubbers and pencils, pencil-sharpeners, bookmarks, and hosts of other things, all bearing an inscription to the ways of the Lord. Prizes were thrown here and there. Charlie Firbag got a rubber which he didn't want, and Hugh McDonnell got a pencil with the message *I am the Way, the Truth, and the Light* printed in gold lettering. Hugh felt a bit peculiar this evening, and very happy to receive this token. He would cherish it, unlike many of the others who eagerly wanted to receive, but who would not cherish the object once obtained. Hugh felt strangely elated. For some time now he had been moving towards this moment and now, the assurance that he would finally accept the Lord Jesus into his heart, filled him with joy. He was excited by the idea that his salvation was imminent.

"Remember children, these are our earthly prizes but they are nothing compared to the riches which the love of God can bring to us. To end this evening, I would like us all to sing 'I'm Happy, Saved and Loved', and I want you all to make a special effort."

The piano struck up without delay and the children set off on one last raucous outburst which exceedingly pleased Mr Hands by its sheer gusto. When finished, he said another prayer and gave a final blessing, at last freeing the children to bustle and joust their way out of the Emmanuel Mission Hall.

Hugh McDonnell was an impressionable child. Before passing through the doors, he once more contemplated the enraptured expression on the face of Mr Hands, and then caught a last glimpse of the broad beams of the arched ceiling. In all his movements he was conscious of his body from the tips of his fingers to the tips of his toes.

As he was sucked into Glenalpen Street he became aware of the night-turning blackness, broken only by the pools of smoky-yellow light pouring out of the public houses, and the burnt glow ringing the gas lamps. There was also a noise—an accordion, in the distance. Three of the Firbags had decided to go round several pubs in order to collect money for the still far-off bonfire, and could be seen lit-up by the smoky light spilling on to them. The children who lived in the immediate vicinity of the Mission soon disappeared into their houses, whilst the others were already dispersing in all directions.

Hugh moved down the street and turned left into Sandy Row which was brightly lit and still busy with cars. The noise of the accordion quickly died out. He turned left again into Albion Street which cut off the noise of the cars and the lights of the Row. As he walked along, the silence was made tangible by the wheezing lamps, broken now and again by a gas spurt of flame. One or two of the houses had been bricked up. Others were dark and looked as if no one lived in them. They made him feel unsafe and alien.

Becoming frightened and feeling very much alone, the boy began walking sideways, turning his back to the protective wall as he moved along the street. He glanced up at the sky. At first he saw only blackness, but as his eyes took in more, he perceived millions of little spots dancing silver here and there. He fancied that he was discovering something strangely beautiful, and his breast expanded. He stopped walking and gazed fixedly at the stars: "Help me Lord Jesus, make me strong. I love you Lord Jesus." He began walking again, bubbling inside. His feet gathered pace until he broke into a dash. He turned right into Kensington Street and kept running until he stood breathless in front of his own house. He looked at the stars once more and said, "Thank you, Lord," before going in.

He found his sister ironing shirts and underclothing in front of the fire. Monday night was her night to do the housework whilst her mother attended the Women's Club off the Shankill Road. Hugh was trying to circumnavigate the ironing board in order to get to the armchair when she asked him calmly to get some coal from the yard, but added more authoritatively, "An' ya bedder get yar pyjamas on before yar mammy comes back."

Hugh went reluctantly into the scullery and then through another door to the toilet outside which also harboured the coal. He took the shovel—which he almost fell over—and blindly plunged it into the darkness. It scraped and sparked along the ground until he could feel the weight upon it.

Hugh stood motionless until his eyes began to adjust to the dark. He could distinguish a few bits of coal which faintly reflected the skylight. The sky came through a gap of about a square foot between the toilet and the scullery. He looked up at the stars which seemed to move constantly as his vision lost itself by concentrating on the immensity of space.

"Let the Lord Jesus come into my heart," he said quietly. It was as if someone else had spoken, and the incongruity of the words upon the silence excited him. His chest began to beat wildly and, as he looked heavenwards, moved in the joy of his own salvation, it seemed as if the stars rained down upon the toilet, playing a crystal melody upon his sensitive skin. All of a sudden, he was pulled out of his rapture by his sister's voice.

"What are ya doin' out there, eh? Ya've left all the doors open 'n there's a draught here wud kill a horse!" Hugh grasped the shovel tightly and hurried in. He tossed the coal on to the almost-extinguished fire without saying anything. His sister looked enquiringly at him, but she got no response.

"Hurry up 'n get up t' bed!" she said, obviously irritated by his silence. It surprised her that he obeyed without objection.

From his bed he could look through the back window to the sky. He felt his being move upwards towards the stars. His sleep that night was tinselled with a sort of celestial dust, and his slumber knitted him into the fabric of another world. When he awoke next morning, it was to the sound of buses and cars struggling and snorting in the gold-turning light which was fusing through the cracked pane of his bedroom window. He dressed, and descended the stairs hurriedly. He found his mother warming her over-garments by the fire. She was preparing for work. Hugh went to her and sat on the carpet between her legs, his back resting lightly against her chair.

"I was saved last night, mammy," he said tranquilly, letting the back of his head drop on to her lap.

"Were ya son? That's great! I just hope ya can keep to it." She pulled her hand over his forehead, catching his front lick of hair and letting it fall randomly. She repeated this unconsciously, running her soft fingers soothingly over his scalp. He relaxed into a world of gentle colours and sounds, slipping momentarily out of the world of the street. The movements of her fingertips installed an atmosphere of gentleness and silence between them and they remained speechless for some time, until he said again:

"Yes, I'm saved nigh …"

She bent forward and kissed his head. Outside, the buses and cars, the Firbags and the world of fits and fevers, cheered, choked, spat, kicked and made yelping Indian noises.

Shit

There was the usual pandemonium in the Blythe Street schoolyard at breaktime: a lot of skipping, jumping and stepping gingerly over boundaries hastily chalked out on the yard tarmac; running and chasing; a disorganised game which involved trying to avoid being hit by a ball of screwed up newspaper; and little groups of children pulling, pushing and trailing each other good-naturedly around in circles. The scene was sprinkled here and there with a few isolated children who were momentarily detached from the multiple goings-on. Hugh was trying to catch sight of Anne Maxwell who had promised earlier that she was going to come round to his street after school. It was for this reason that he refused to get roped into the ball game which McCurley had tried desperately to get him involved with.

He wasn't quite sure why he was running after Anne. She was a year older than him and in Mrs Burns' P.9 class. Everyone knew that she 'fancied him', which flattered him because it was very unusual for an older girl to want to go out with a boy in a lower year. Hugh was both excited and afraid, because he didn't really know what was going to be expected of him, and only vaguely what it meant to be 'going out' with someone. But Anne was very pretty.

As Hugh searched unsuccessfully for the girl, the bell rang to announce the end of breaktime. Its loud metallic drone smothered the screaming noises in the yard until the latter fell reluctantly into subdued obedience. When the dumb vibrations ceased, a numbed and surprised silence fell, like that following the sudden swoop out to sea of a crowd of rowdy gulls. The children moved up the steps of the primary school and began filing along the corridor until they eventually filtered into their respective classrooms. Mrs Copeland had P.8 and her room was on the ground floor which meant that once the pupils were through the large wooden entrance doors, they were quickly in their classroom and at their desks. Mrs Copeland was a middle-aged woman with very sharp features whose kindness to the children took the protective form of curt inquisitiveness which frequently verged on the brutal. The day before, she had asked her pupils to bring in as many different leaves as they could find. Sandy Row not being one of the leafier areas of Belfast, the harvest she had in front of her was disappointingly poor to say the least. Fortunately she had taken the precaution to come equipped with an array of oak, elm, chestnut, and other leaves more easily found in her part of the city. Thus armed, she began her last lesson of the day on the exotic topic of trees.

The afternoon was bright and the classroom warm. Slanting rays of sunlight lit up the nature charts Mrs Copeland had put at the front of the class. Certain leaves were bold and stood out against the light whilst others were translucent and veined and made some of the children uncomfortable. But the natural colours were attractive and unusual to them. Mrs Copeland began to teach in her own idiosyncratic way: going off in long, winding monologues which would be suddenly punctuated by a salve of quick and piercing questions. Inevitably, the dreamy and unarmed child would be annihilated by her unexpected thrusts. And when an answer did not return as rapidly as the question had been fired off, Mrs Copeland would become cross; then she would redden and become confused. Her evenings were often spent in self-recriminations as she sat lonely and disappointed at the fireside with what she was sensitive enough to consider as her own failings.

Hugh sat with his gaze fixed on some brown, fuzzy-looking pouches and shiny-green, beetle-like glands on one of the educational posters pinned to the blackboard, his head propped up by his hands, and his mind floating off into the late-afternoon meeting with Anne. He hoped she wouldn't be wearing skates. He hated girls on skates. He had a vision of her turning round and round him in circles. Hateful. His mind was slowly brought back into his present surroundings by a partly painful, partly pleasant stirring in his bowels which bestowed upon him the uncomfortable realisation that in his endeavours to find Anne at breaktime, he had forgotten to go to the toilet. He had of course meant to, but the problem had not had its present urgency. He looked at Mrs Copeland who was hopelessly lost in branches and trees. He could expect nothing from her. In fact, Mrs Copeland was very strict about such matters: children were to go only at break or lunchtimes, and certainly not during class. Hugh began to fidget.

Mrs Copeland suddenly became aware of the boy because of what she recognised irritably as shuffling. She made a mercilessly clinical thrust at him: "Repeat what I have just said, Hugh." The teacher looked at her pupil with tiny, tight-beaded eyes. She was brandishing an acorn in her left hand which she covered with her fingers. It seemed to him that he had heard the word 'seed'.

"You were talking about seeds Miss," he ventured.

"What about them?" she aimed a second, clean thrust at him. The boy went momentarily dumb. Then from somewhere hidden in his consciousness he dragged up a few words:

"About becoming trees, Miss." His voice was hesitant and she was tempted to go for him again. She scrutinised his open face and decided to accept his answer. It wasn't exactly what she had said, but close enough for the others to be confused about its exactitude. Mrs Copeland was just about to cut him out of her attention when, encouraged by his success, Hugh went on courageously, "Can I go to the toilet Miss?"

She scrutinised the frayed ends of the dirty cuffs of his shirt, her dark eyes becoming black. "No! You cannot," she replied firmly.

Hugh was becoming very ill at ease. He closed his eyes and fixed his concentration on the control of his body, but it was a struggle which he knew he could not win. He began to transpire profusely. Mrs Copeland abandoned him and went on with her fruits and seeds, acorns and oak trees, whilst the rest of the class made an effort every now and then to rise out of the milky warmth of the afternoon. The pupils were vaguely conscious that an act of attention was necessary in order not to be skewered unawares by one of Mrs Copeland's nervous thrusts. The latter suddenly suspended one of her characteristic flights of irrelevantly poetic explanations of the natural world in order to observe Hugh's unnaturally immobile body. The boy sat planted, rigid and flushed.

"What's wrong with you McDonnell?" Seeing his enflamed face, she tempered the offence of his surname by a more sympathetic tone: "Are you alright?"

Hugh was not alright. He sat mortified, as if a flame was slowly devouring him.

"Can I go to the toilet, Miss?" was his answer to her enquiry. He did not look at the woman. Her immediate inclination was to correct his 'can' by 'may', but after satisfying herself that something was seriously wrong with the boy she accepted to put aside the pedagogy, albeit for the second time.

"Go on," came the magnanimous reply.

The boy rose mechanically from his chair. That was the easy part. He moved apprehensively towards the door, trailing his legs as if he no longer had joints at the knees. All the eyes of the class were upon him. The silence was tactfully shattered by the teacher's clap of the hands which brought all eyes to the front and allowed the boy to escape through the classroom door. On the other side, Hugh was relieved to hear that Mrs Copeland had launched once again into her categorisation of fruits and seeds.

Hugh was absent for a considerable length of time, and when he returned, he stood for a moment against the wall, listening at the classroom door. The lesson had moved on to the reading of a poem. Hugh felt more composed. But on opening the door, he unintentionally cut Mrs Copeland in the middle of a sentence. The two exchanged glances, but the boy's eyes were furtive and refused any lengthy contact. That refusal was sufficiently informative for the woman not to make any comment, and the boy discreetly crept to his seat.

Not much remained of the afternoon lesson before the final alarmed ringing of the bell which shattered the peace which had settled upon the class. Mrs Copeland gratefully released her children who began to recover and push their way to the door. Hugh held back until they had all left the room, feigning to put his desk in order. Then he too was out of the room before his teacher had become conscious of his presence. He moved quickly and had soon passed through the large wooden doors and finally through the school gates. He weaved in and out of little groups of pupils from other classes who were making their way through the labyrinth of streets which ran off Blythe Street. When there were few remaining in front of him he broke into a run which took him obliviously past cars and houses until he crossed Sandy Row into the secure warren of the streets which made up his home territory. He was aware only of his burning cheeks and forehead.

When he reached his house, his mother was struggling with the washing in what they called the 'outhouse', which was the kitchen, dinning room, bathroom, washroom, and work-shed, all combined in an area of about three feet by eight feet. He was spared the trial of her seeing him. He climbed the steep stairs to his bedroom and threw himself face down on the bed were he lay inert for what seemed to him like a long time, not daring to move. The realisation that he had to see Anne at five o'clock outside the Orange Hall began to permeate his consciousness until it took sole possession of his thoughts and filled him with fear and panic. He rose quickly and went downstairs where he relievedly found the house empty; washed himself and then put on clean, but non-ironed clothes which his mother had folded and left stacked beside the linen basket. He went out again into the street which he looked down in a sort of resentful conspiracy. He decided to walk round by Stroud Street rather than take the shortest route via the busy Donegall Road. He passed uninviting doorways and blank windows of unused parlours. It was surprising that in such tiny, overcrowded houses a whole room was left just an unused, but comparatively well-furnished space.

Hugh became aware of someone looking at him. Tommy Firbag senior had just stepped out of the bookies across the street and had obviously quickened his stride in order to catch up with the young lad. Tommy's son Sammy was in the same class as

Hugh. Sammy was a lot like his father, not yet just as uncouth and challenging, although the potential was certainly there.

"Hear ya shit yarself taday, Hughey boy, eh?"

Hugh looked up at the tall, grimy and vulgar-looking man, but did not answer him. For an instant he looked into the half-amused, mocking eyes, but on reaching Stroud Street, turned abruptly left to leave the man at a bit of a loss. Tommy gazed at the back of the boy and after a somewhat forced laugh of derision he added:

"Happens ta th' best of us, son!" but Hugh did not look back.

Hugh walked on quickly past the brick walls of the backyards which afforded him protection from the eyes of the street. He crossed Wesley Street and then turned left into Combermere Street. The top half of this street was curious in that he knew no one who lived there because the families who now occupied these houses had no children of his age. It was a different generation—that of his brothers and sisters—and the children had grown up and moved away to housing estates in a different part of the city. The top of Combermere Street looked cleaner than elsewhere and above all, contained no apparent danger, no risk.

He reached the top of the street, crossed through the noise and the cars and buses of the Donegall Road, then turned into the top part of Sandy Row. Anne was already waiting for him. He could see her holding on to the window ledge of the Orange Hall. Not only was she wearing roller skates, but she was accompanied by another, bespectacled girl, who was also wearing roller skates. Hugh's heart sank and a wave of revulsion ran over him. But he continued to advance as it was the only course of action which he considered acceptable at this point.

As he approached, he saw that they recognised him, for they began to perform strange body contortions on their skates. When he got close to the girls, they started to move teasingly away, but at a rhythm which meant that they wanted him to catch them up. In spite of himself, Hugh broke into a trot until he cornered both of them at the top of the Row. They clumsily took shelter in a derelict shop entrance. Hugh hesitated, but then joined them in the relative seclusion and quiet provided by this harbour off the street. Hugh intended to say something, but was put off by the girls' giggling. He looked at them and said nothing and the three remained that way for what seemed like an eternity until, all of a sudden, the bespectacled girl, whose name was Marjory, looked at him challengingly and said: "Why don't ya give Anne a kiss?" They both giggled again at this audacity, but the way Anne looked at him made him think that she was waiting expectantly for him to carry out the dare.

Hugh made no advance. The girls then suddenly decided to brush past him and shove off on their skates again. Hugh already felt that he had had enough, but nevertheless decided to follow them once more. This time he was at pains to catch them up. Seeing this, the girls turned into the street which ran along the side of the Orange Hall, and came to an abrupt halt in the side entrance to the latter. Hugh blocked them in again. This time he was feeling audacious and also wanting to hit back at Marjory.

"What did ya bring her for?" he asked Anne, nodding towards the other girl.

"'Cause she's my chum … we're always together." Marjory began to giggle again. She knew that she was irritating him. Her giggle ended in a malicious smile. Then, having waited for her moment, she asked, "Is it true ya went in yar trousers taday?"

"Don't be stupid!" Hugh bitingly replied.

"Is it true?" asked Anne, more concernedly.

He hesitated, then answered calmly "No, it's not true."

"Linda Hilditch said ya did," came the renewed taunt from the bespectacled one.

"She's a liar," said Hugh categorically.

Marjory giggled again, but Anne was not giggling. She looked straight at Hugh and said, "Linda Hilditch told us on the way home that ya did. Sh' said ya cud hardly walk." Anne was secretly hoping that the allegation could be refuted beyond any shadow of a doubt.

"Linda Hilditch's a liar. She's always makin' things up about people."

The girls knew that the last remark was true, but they were certainly not convinced.

"I nearly did … Copie wouldn't let me go to the toilet but I didn't."

Marjory felt that she should temporarily let the subject drop. She grabbed her friend's sleeve and they went off skating again down the street. Hugh watched them without moving. They expected him to follow, but a feeling of revulsion began to take possession of him. He made up his mind to go home, and, after staring fixedly at the girls for several seconds, he turned determinedly away from them. When they realised what he was doing, they decided to follow him. As he reached the corner of the Orange Hall, he could hear their skates stop abruptly behind him. He turned round.

"Where are ya goin'?" asked Anne.

"Home." Before she could say anything else, he distanced himself from them in a way which discouraged any idea of pursuit. He thought he could hear Marjory giggle again, but he was soon out of earshot. He felt relieved on reaching Combermere Street. His brisk pace slowed. He turned reluctantly into Stroud Street and ran his hand along the rough brick walls as he proceeded forward. He felt decidedly unwell, and his mouth was dry and ashen. He would wait a long time before going out with a girl.

As he walked up Kensington Street to number 45, he checked several times that no one was looking at him. When he reached his doorstep he turned bitterly to look down the length of the gaping doorways.

"Shit!" he said, under his breath.

Dumb Show

Hugh McDonnell followed the same itinerary everyday to school. He turned into Stroud Street, crossed Sandy Row, and then followed Blythe Street to its extremity which relievedly opened up into Blythefield Primary School. The itinerary was usually an insouciant one, punctuated by skimming walls, avoiding cracks or lines in the pavement slabs, and pretending that he could fly from one street corner to the next. The latter entailed accelerating, elbows wide, from one kerb to the other, frantically threshing the air in the process. At the age of nine, Hugh believed that he could fly.

This morning was different from other mornings at school. After assembly, Miss MacNamarra made the children of P.9 line up outside the Assembly Hall. She sat at the piano and had them enter one after the other, each pupil closing the door reverently behind them. She had not told the children the purpose of the exceptional circumstances surrounding these early morning theatrics and would not tell them until she had secured the means to follow through with her enterprise. The first step was to establish a school choir, but for the time being the essential participants were to know nothing of the why and the wherefore.

Hugh entered the voluminous hall, which was also the theatre of his footballing successes as well as his more ignominious gymnastic feats, and took up position beside the veneered piano which squatted below the stage at an equidistance from the walls. Miss MacNamarra smiled reassuringly at him. She handed him a song sheet. Straight-backed and hands poised for the kill, she indicated to Hugh from her starched and perched position that he would begin singing the well-known refrain as soon as she began playing. After an abortive first attempt when no vocal sound came forth, Miss MacNamarra recovered her equanimity and proceeded as before. This time a high-pitched, almost melodious timbre followed the piano notes at a respectably secure distance which encouraged the pianist to pigeon-hole the vocalist, if not in the 'definite' category, then at least in the 'promising'. Hugh filtered out of the hall and ushered the next candidate in.

For Miss MacNamarra, the morning passed in a regimental monotony but at the end of it she had very definite convictions as to the outcome of the events. Consequently, she decided to take up the challenge and enter Blythefield Primary School for the annual Northern Ireland Primary School Choir Competition.

It was an event which took place each year in December. This gave her three months to select her pupils and to drill them in the two songs they would perform. She would work initially during school hours and then, from November onwards, remain with the choir for about an hour after school finished for the day, first twice, then three times a week.

The piano remained permanently in the front corner of the Assembly Hall and accompanied the children in morning singing as well as other more infrequent events. Miss MacNamarra, who was thirty-seven and no longer obsessed by remaining a Miss for the rest of her life, decided that she would give herself completely to the children and make it a point of honour to bring a trophy to Sandy Row.

Miss MacNamarra was born on the Malone Road, which was also where she now lived. Nothing seemed to have singled her out to teach in a working-class area of protestant Belfast but now that she had been posted there she was determined to take up the challenge and raise the level of the children to meet her own expectations. Her soul was music. She had begun piano at the age of seven and moved on to other instruments but always returning to what she felt was the only instrument to communicate the values capable of freeing the human spirit from its earthly bondage. She would labour at teaching the children maths and English, but the daily music lesson would be the moment when her function in life would fuse with her desire to rewrite the unfair constitution of the human predicament. The choir of about 30 tender souls from the 120 children who made up P.9–P.11 would compose her chosen battalion which would go forth and vindicate her lifelong calling. To this end she dedicated her coffee and lunch breaks during the month of September.

When she had composed what she felt to be more or less the elite of her troops, Miss MacNamarra organised the twice-weekly practice sessions to prepare the children for the coming winter ordeal. The first practices went well enough. It was a matter of installing discipline and reverence amongst the children and bringing them to a point of familiarisation with the piano and her own idiosyncratic signals for embarking, drawing out, and concluding the pieces on the programme. The initial training accomplished, Miss MacNamarra concentrated on producing a harmonious ensemble which sought a tentative balance between enthusiasm and competence. And it was this enterprise which was to produce her major handicap. After two or three weeks of cajoling and pushing the various elements into line, it became obvious to her that a strident, grating timbre was consistently either one step ahead or one step behind, below or above, the other members of the choir. Her well-trained ear homed in on the top right-hand corner of the beaming faces before her.

Hugh McDonnell was tall for his age and had been suitably placed with the older pupils of P.10 and P.11 who made up the back row of the choir. He had not been convinced by his selection that he had a commendable singing voice. No one had ever previously remarked upon his newly-revealed talent and it was with an unsure footing that he took up his place in the back row of Blythefield Primary School Choir. Nevertheless, he was obediently programmed to give of his best.

When it became apparent to the more sensitive children that something was not absolutely as it should have been, Hugh immediately began to doubt the appropriateness of his selection. When Miss MacNamarra's attention turned conspicuously in the direction of his whereabouts, Hugh became possessed by a panic which he had not experienced before. It soon became obvious that the teacher's attention was irrevocably turned towards the top right-hand corner of the choir which would quickly be called to publically justify its selection.

Miss MacNamarra feigned not to be overly interested in the group of children on her right. After all, she had selected them, albeit hastily, and was most concerned that no child would feel in any way excluded on her account. Her own father had made her life extremely trying by forcing numerous embarrassing moments upon her and it was far from her desire to inflict a similar degrading experience on any child in her care. She refused to oblige the children to sing individually in front of their peers. Consequently, she proceeded methodically by selecting a group of five and asking them to sing the last lines of their second song. The result was relatively convincing and the teacher moved on to another group of five songsters. Hugh had a good idea that he was the target of her investigation. When it came to his group of five, instead of singing out enthusiastically with the others, he simply mimed the words. He opened his mouth and pushed forth the air which had accumulated in his lungs, and even accompanied his gesture with a facial expression which convinced Miss MacNamarra that he was obviously participating to the full. After going through all the members on the right-hand side of the choir, the puzzled teacher left off and decided that she must have been listening on a different register or that her hearing had been contaminated by the poor sound quality of the room or the noises from the road and railway line not far off.

The form-teacher of P.9 and ardent music lover resumed the normal choir-practice and over the next two weeks she was well rewarded for her endeavours as the group of children could be heard to make substantial progress. It just so happened that during this time Hugh, almost fully persuaded that he was the strange note in the otherwise relatively harmonious ensemble, had resolved to continue bravely with his solitary and convincing act of dumb mimicry.

Jane Milligan was a year older than Hugh and stood beside him in the back line of the choir. As the practice sessions continued, an acknowledged attraction developed between the two children. They were on the verge of going out together, prevented only by the stigma attached to the fact that Jane was a year older than the boy. But as the afternoon repetitions increased in number the two were drawn inevitably together.

When the sessions moved into November and the darkness fell early on Blythe Street, singling the choir out from the world which surrounded them, Hugh was on the point of asking Jane to 'go out' with him. The latter did not really involve going anywhere in particular but simply seeing each other perhaps one evening a week after school. Nevertheless, the decision was monumental and Hugh had to work up the courage to bring it to a successful conclusion.

As he stood beside the eloquent silhouette of the young girl to his left, Hugh decided that it would be directly after this first November choir practice, when he could corner her briefly and secretly before she escaped home. He looked distractedly at her immaculate profile as she confidently filled her lungs in response to Miss MacNamarra's timely beckoning. In an instant of infectious enthusiasm he let himself be drawn into the movement of her sonorous utterance and allowed himself to break into song. The result was not lost upon the music teacher who had already moved from the piano and stood herself conspicuously before the children in order to fit their participation all the better into a taut time frame.

Miss MacNamarra dropped her arms suddenly as if their life supply had just been cut off. This had the immediate result of numbing the children to an incomprehensible drone. She looked suspiciously at the top right-hand corner of the choir. This time, she could not let the culprit escape.

"I'm sorry children but I have a little problem of articulation coming from the back row there. I wonder if you three at the back could sing the first two lines for me, one after the other? Jane, you begin."

Miss MacNamarra led the girl through the lines and nodded to her approvingly. "Now you, Hugh …" She moved her hands invitingly towards him. Hugh became flustered but controlled himself well and managed to perform the lines with just less than moderate success. Miss MacNamarra made no remark and looked immediately at the boy on Hugh's left who was similarly invited to repeat the lines. This task finished, Miss MacNamarra resumed the session without further demonstration. Hugh breathed deeply and moved back into his dumb but extravagant show. He showed outward calm but decided to abandon asking Jane to go out with him.

The morning after this session, the children played normally in the schoolyard awaiting the bell to call them into class. Miss MacNamarra took this opportunity to single out Hugh from the others and ask him to help her arrange the desks in the classroom. Hugh followed obediently but not without a suspicion that something was wrong and that he was about to find out just what. When they had entered the classroom, Hugh's suspicions were quickly confirmed. His schoolteacher began apprehensively:

"Hugh, I know that we have been practicing now for some time … and that you have been a ready participant … but, I just wanted to ask you … you haven't always been participating fully, have you? I mean, I think that sometimes you have been pretending to sing, isn't that right?"

The boy moved his body weight from one leg to the other. It was no use pretending, besides he wasn't sure that he wanted to continue with the choir anyway.

"Yes, Miss," he replied, whilst looking out of the windows towards the schoolyard.

"You know Hugh, sometimes a boy's voice can change early and unexpectedly … there can be many reasons … I'm not quite sure what happened in this case. But anyway, never mind." Miss MacNamarra hesitated. She did not want the boy to lose face as far as the other children were concerned. It seemed to her that he had already made a big effort in coming to all the practice sessions and she did not want to disappoint him. After a silent interval, she turned to Hugh and said:

"Look Hugh, this is what I want you to do. I want you to continue coming to the choir—there isn't much time to go before the competition, so I would like you to continue to come, but," here she hesitated as much out of pedagogical interests as out of her feeling for the young pupil, "I would like you to continue miming. I would like you to continue pretending to sing—especially on the day of the competition—do you think that you could do that for me?"

Unsure of what he should be feeling, Hugh looked at her and said quietly "Yes, Miss."

"Well then, go back to the playground and we will pretend that this little meeting never took place, alright?" Hugh shook his head appropriately and began moving towards the door of the classroom.

Subsequent choir practice sessions became increasingly uncomfortable for the boy, partly because of the miming which was now semi-officialised, and partly because of the strange, silent relationship which was established between teacher and pupil. His non-relationship with Jane was curiously suspended as if they were waiting for something to happen which would bring them together. Fortunately, he did not have to put up with the growing discomfort for very long as they were soon into December and on the eve of the competition itself.

As the tension built up before the event, all of the pupils became intensely excited. All, except Hugh, who showed no sign of nerves and seemed to remain surprisingly aloof, enclosed within his own private little bubble. His extraordinary calm was not lost on the others who were paradoxically more attracted to him.

On the celebrated day, the thirty-odd children, along with three or four members of the staff of Blythefield Primary School, were taken by coach to the seaside resort of Bangor and deposited ceremoniously in front of an imposing building which had seen better days as a theatre but, from the posters on the walls, was now precariously functioning as a cinema. Along with many other groups of children easily distinguished by their school uniforms, the Blythefield children swarmed through the front doors into the impressive volumes within, and took up seats in specially delegated areas of the building.

Before they could perform, they were obliged to listen to around thirty other choirs from all parts of the province. The discipline of these groups, along with the obvious quality of their uniforms, made an impression on the Sandy Row children which Miss MacNamarra and her colleagues were quick to underline and praise. They would try to make capital out of it in the days ahead.

When their turn came, the children and their music teacher filed up the narrow side steps on to the stage and took up their usual banana shape around the woman who would lead them into their pieces but not accompany them on the piano as this had to be done by a lady who had been designated to carry out this important task. The performance went well: Hugh mimed convincingly and the children went through their drill with a confidence and enthusiasm which compensated for a more secondary lack of polish.

After excitedly and relievedly taking up their seats again, the party had to sit through another dozen or so performances before the judging could begin. The latter was a relatively rapid affair with the winning schools designated in reverse order. The children were disappointed not to be named, but as they looked perplexedly at Miss MacNamarra there followed another announcement that a special prize had been awarded to Blythefield Primary School. No one was really sure what this prize had been awarded for but it was quickly decided by Miss MacNamarra that Hugh would go to the stage to receive it. Suddenly, the latter became affected by the official nature of the situation. He managed to climb the steps without mishap but when presented with the modest silver trophy, was unable even to say 'thank you', which caused the presenter of the award to stare after the boy asking himself whether or not the judges had done the right thing. Hugh brought the trophy back to his teacher who received it with a knowing smile at the boy.

Just before the Christmas holidays, the members of the choir were individually presented with a certificate testifying to their participation in the grand event and stating that the school had been the recipient of the famous 'special award' which still no one knew—and no one questioned—the reason for. Hugh did not give the certificate to his mother, but left it negligently in his schoolbag until it was found by Mrs McDonnell when emptying the satchel to prepare it for the next term.

"You didn't tell me you won a certificate for the singin'," she smiled proudly to her son when he came in from the street. But his expression quickly made her satisfaction change to concern.

"What's wrong with you?" she asked. Hugh shrugged his shoulders. "Are you nat happy to get a certificate?" Hugh looked away.

"C'mon, what's wrong?" she said encouragingly. But Hugh would not talk about it. He looked at the certificate lying on the wee table against the wall. He seemed to burn his eyes on it. He quickly glanced away.

"Nothin'," was all he said and his mother knew when he closed up like that that it would do no good to continue the subject today. Her conversation turned instead to preparations for Christmas which she knew he would be happy to share.

After the Christmas holidays, Miss MacNamarra was keen to continue with the school choir. The preparations for the competition, as well as the result of the event itself, had created a good atmosphere amongst the children and given the school a sense of cohesion. They would be able to sing on important assembly days—religious festivals and end of term celebrations. She asked them all to meet as usual around the piano in the hall. Hugh was noticeably absent, which of course did not surprise her. Unknown to her, Hugh had resolved never to sing again in public. He felt that he had cheated, and the fact that the school, through Miss MacNamarra, sanctioned the tromperie, made it all the more difficult to accept. His confidence in himself and those around him had been shaken.

Several uneventful weeks passed. At the beginning of February, the children arrived in class to find a severe looking, thin, mustachioed man sitting at the back of the room. He was an inspector come to see how Miss MacNamarra was progressing with the children of P.9. The teacher cautiously remained on well-trodden ground, going over a botany lesson they had already covered the week before. She cleverly guided the children, soliciting answers they were very willing to give, being only too happy to show off the knowledge they possessed in front of an obviously important visitor. In the spate of enthusiastic hand-raising which accompanied an unruly hiss of "Miss," the stranger noticed that a boy at the front was not participating. He stood up quietly and moved towards Hugh's table. The classroom became silent. The man addressed the boy directly:

"Don't you know the name of that yellow flower your teacher is showing you?" But Hugh did not answer. He looked at the card held in front of the class. The inspector was not used to such silence from a nine-year-old and wondered whether or not the boy had some physical or mental problem.

"What's your name, boy?" The tone of the question was more inquisitive than gentle. Hugh looked down at his desk and mumbled his name. It was painful for him to say it.

"What did you say, boy, speak up."

"Hugh, sir," but again, he was barely audible.

"Joseph?" the man enquired disbelievingly.

"Hugh."

"You! Your name is 'You'! First time I've met anyone called 'You'." The man paused to appreciate the giggles he knew his joke would provoke.

"Hugh," this time the boy aspirated the *h*, but the scene was proving to be an intolerable ordeal for him. The inspector approached the teacher and discreetly remarked that the boy must always sit at the front because he was obviously disruptive and she could keep her eye on him there. Miss MacNamarra calmly but firmly refuted these remarks and went on to confirm that Hugh was one of the most intelligent members of the class but added that he was a sensitive boy and that it would perhaps be better not to insist upon things just at this point. The inspector acquiesced and took up his place once again at the back of the class. He was nevertheless more unwilling to look upon the teacher's conduct of the class in a favourable light. He sat out the time until the bell rang for break silently making notes. During the break, he subsequently proceeded to tell the teacher the numerous failings of her lesson.

When class resumed, no more was said of the matter. Miss MacNamarra for the most part avoided direct eye-contact with the boy. For his part, Hugh spent the rest of the day refusing to participate verbally in the class. He would say nothing, but at the same time he burned with the desire to contribute to the events going on around him.

Ironies

Red, Oscar, Smiley, Don and Hugh set out about three in the afternoon. It was a summer day and the air hung heavy with a bright, warm blueness. Hugh's eleventh birthday had just passed and coincided this year with the first day of the school holiday. The 'good weather' had just alighted on Sandy Row. Hugh did not care a lot for the heat as it made him feel ill, but for the moment, it was very much of a novelty and so he was glad to feel the warmth on his head; glad to feel the sun on his black curly hair.

It had been too warm to stay in the street today. Where the road had been repaired, the little black pools of tarmac were becoming soft and sticky and giving off a nauseating odour. All the boys had felt the same irritating monotony as they had sat on the pavement under the sun which had made them feel out of place in the street. And the street had responded by disowning them and pushing them out into the afternoon. There had been no need to vote which direction they would take off in: they needed crisper air and greenness.

So at about three o'clock, they set off in the direction of the Botanic Gardens, to go rummaging or 'plundering', as Red liked to call it. Despite the heat, they made their way enthusiastically up Botanic Avenue: bobbing in and out of trees; pulling the drawers of cigarette machines; ransacking phone boxes; prodding or poking at anything which might hold a suspicion of interest or gain. When they decided to play follow-my-leader, Hugh was a little hesitant as he was not particularly adept at jumping or climbing. It would be alright as long as he stayed at the rear and pretended to do exactly the same as the others. But the others were aware of his apprehension. They let him come along because he was considered to be smart and came up with some good ideas, but on the whole they kept somewhat aloof from him and sometimes made him feel excluded.

Red was the natural, self-appointed leader. He was fifteen and bigger than the others. Even though he wore glasses, his wild spirit earned him the respect of everyone. In a curious way he was drawn to Hugh, but he did not really like him. Red led the file of five boys which followed the whims of its leader over the bonnets of cars and postboxes, swinging from low branches in the tree-lined avenue. Things were going fine until they reached the line of terraced houses. Red began walking along the narrow walls encompassing the gardens, and then jumped the gaps between the pillars of the gates, scooping off the heads of any unfortunate flowers which found themselves in his path. The others followed closely behind, but Hugh held back at the gates. He waited until he thought the others were not looking and then descended from the wall and followed them swiftly along the pavement until he could join them on the wall again. He half-heartedly swiped at a few flowers just to show his good intentions, and the others pretended not to have noticed that he had not done exactly as they had.

Oscar, Smiley and Don began talking eagerly about visiting a 'den'—a place the three had discovered on a previous outing in the same direction. The boys had many dens. These were secret places where you could find things which had no apparent owner, or that nobody seemed to be attending to. Thus they had strawberry dens and cherry dens, along with others where you could find bamboo canes or apples or sometimes even toys or bicycles. Of course, they could never bring the bicycles home to keep, but they could simply borrow them to get home with and then abandon them close by. Hugh did not know where any of these dens could be found. He was interested in the bamboo den, but pretended not to be. The others would not tell him anything, especially if he asked. To know lots of dens was a way of earning the highest respect, and secrets were jealously kept. Only Red knew virtually every den. Hugh began to worry that he was going to be left on his own, that he would have to walk back alone, for Red now joined in the whispering about the bamboo den. Hugh realised painfully that he was not essential to today's venture.

Fortunately, the conversation was brought to an abrupt halt when Oscar, always the most observant of his surroundings, espied a young woman walking towards them. She was probably a student, in her early twenties, blond-haired and very well-built.

"I bet ya I cud squeeze her tits," said Oscar, proudly looking up at Red.

"Let's see ya then," challenged the latter.

Immediately Oscar started off nonchalantly towards the unsuspecting female whilst the other boys stood off in anticipation. When he broke into a trot, the others took refuge behind a car parked conveniently nearby. Oscar gathered momentum, and as he ran he focused his vision straight in front of him, feigning not to be in the least interested in the young woman who was carrying two or three books under her right arm. When he was almost upon her, he jumped into the air and thrust his hand forward onto her left breast. The other boys gaped and gasped and giggled in admiration. The young woman squealed. Before she had time to turn her head after him, Oscar was racing heroically up the avenue. She was completely at a loss. Her breath was cut and her chest was wrung with fury and frustration. Out of her enraged confusion came a fierce and bitter cry: "Beast! Bloody little animal, that's all you are!"

Red and the others looked on fascinated and excited. They decided to avoid the young woman, who had begun to walk shakily towards them, by scattering up an alley on the other side of the road. By turning right and then right again, they came out further up the avenue where they found Oscar waiting on the corner.

"Did yis see the bumpers on 'er?" he asked, trying to get his breath back. But the others wanted to get away as quickly as possible from the scene of the crime, and since they were now close to the back of the university, Red said:

"Come on … let's get into the gardies."

Hugh, although he had disliked the episode, was well pleased that the bamboo den had momentarily slipped out of their preoccupations. Since he had, in a way, participated as much as the others—except Oscar— in the adventure, he felt integrated and relieved.

The five passed the huge dark-green and gold-topped gates of the Botanic Gardens, and entered the park which they found surprisingly deserted. A few old men and women sat like die-cast figures on benches overlooking the vast green field. Most of the old people sat absolutely motionless: one or two sat with their mouths partly open as if they had forgotten the end of their sentence; another sat arched on the bench as if he had just dropped something but was unable to bend further to pick it up. They remained indifferent to the arrival of the boys and did not stir out of their numb stillness, whilst to the boys, the static figures were no more than suspended wafts of grey, poised magically in the shadow of the blue air.

"Where d' ya wanna go nigh?" said Oscar in his tireless enthusiasm, "… to the Glass House?" and he nodded over towards the Palm House whose dome glittered enticingly above the shrubs and trees.

"No," said Red, eager to regain control over the party, "it's too fuckin' hat in there … let's go through the puzzies."

The Puzzle-Walk was a collection of plants and trees densely grouped and landscaped with mounds and hollows which were looped with narrow paths. Some of the trees had grown unusually high, so that the entire area remained sombre even in midsummer. To the boys, it was darkest Africa. Even Red, despite his age, was invaded by the impression that they had entered a far off, tropical kingdom where anything might happen, where they might stumble over any amount of plunder.

After making sure that the park keeper was nowhere in sight, they left the narrow path they had been following and made their way into the thick clumps of trees and bushes. They had to crawl flat on their bellies and were inevitably scratched and torn. Hugh was particularly awkward at this and, after having fallen behind, he decided to go back the way he had come and then follow another path to the other side of the Puzzle-Walk near the rose bushes, where he expected the boys to emerge. He did this, but they did not emerge there. Hugh waited, half-hidden behind a tree. He could hear no sound save the noise of some birds swirling around the bandstand. As minutes went on, he became invaded by a devastating feeling of isolation.

Suddenly, it seemed to him that he could hear them whistling and hooting a good distance over to the right. There was no doubt in his mind, they were on their way to the bowling green. Hugh craftily took another path in order to head them off, at the same time preparing some fabulation to meet them with. But when he caught up, they pretended not to notice that he had been absent. Red stopped to gaze across the bowling green to the playing fields beyond which gave on to the Ormeau Embankment. There was no one to be seen, certainly no one playing football.

"Where are all the bastards hidin' today?" he asked in a tone of genuine disappointment.

"I need a piss ..." was all that Don could contribute. And he was about to relieve himself on the spot when the park keeper's whistle blasted out fiercely not far from them. They walked off innocently towards what remained of the changing-block which they knew had a toilet at the far end.

The changing-huts were part of an old wooden edifice with an uninspiring rusty corrugated-iron roof. Once safely behind the building, Don relieved himself by sending a golden arc through the sunny air. He delighted in scattering the arc in broken splashes against the wall.

Red put Oscar's back against the wall, using him as a ladder to get on to the roof. Next up was Smiley, followed by Don and Hugh, who also had to be pulled up by Red. Oscar managed to scramble up by his own means. The five picked their steps gingerly as they moved across the flimsy metal roof which was hot from the sunshine. For some time now the building had stopped being a solid construction or even offering efficient protection from the rain. Despite the metal, their tentative movements made little noise. As they approached the toilet from above—it was the only part of the building which did not have a roof—Red motioned with his hand for them all to stop.

"Did ya hear that?" he asked of Smiley, who was closest to him.

"What?" returned Oscar, having caught his words.

There was a low, scraping sound, dull—like something being rubbed repeatedly against the wall.

"Somebody havin' a crap," said Oscar, beaming radiantly.

"Shut yar mouth!" said Red, with the authority only he could command.

The boys crouched in silence. They were intrigued by other sounds now coming from one of the cubicles. Cautiously, they manoeuvred themselves on to the lavatory wall which overlooked the four partially-covered toilets.

It was the high heat of the afternoon, and the warmth wafted the smell of urine into the air. The smell was familiar and only partly nauseating. There was a heavy drone of flies which seemed unnaturally loud. The boys leaned forward as far as possible until they could see into the dingy cabinet. Two eyes, small and stretched, reached out like two antennae from the semi-darkness. They distinguished the silhouette of a man pressed tightly against the wall, groaning, seeming as if he was trying to communicate something.

"What's 'e doin'?" asked Smiley, the youngest of the boys.

"'E's havin' a wank, the dirty oul bastard!" said Red, half-laughing. Then in a louder voice that the person in the cubicle could hear, he put in a challenging question:

"Ha much'll ya give us if w' wank ya off?"

The man did not answer, but stepped smartly back into the shadow, retracting like some weird sea-creature back into its shell. Red and Oscar hastily descended cistern pipes into the urinal, and stood defiantly at the toilet door. The others, perched above, listened attentively as a bar was slid across the door which then opened slightly. Hugh was able to catch snippets from phrases which were harshly, brokenly, delivered. Something to do with shillings and ball bearings.

"What's 'e sayin'?" asked Smiley, who was a bit hard of hearing.

"'E says 'e'll give us some ironies," Oscar shouted up to the three left on the wall.

The door opened a little further—just sufficiently to suck Red and Oscar into the obscurity. Don and Smiley shimmied hurriedly down the pipes while Hugh remained perched on the wall. As he sat alone, his eyes took in the horizon. He looked across the fields to his left, to the traffic and humming noises beyond. From the wall he could see the bridge over the Lagan River, but could not see the water. The wind blew warmly into his body, billowing his shirt and making him feel insecure on the wall. Despite the warm wind, he began to feel chilly, and perhaps a little frightened. He decided to climb down, and began moving awkwardly backwards, bit by bit until he reached the slanting roof. Smiley saw him and called out, "Where d' ya think yar goin' … it's yar turn next!"

Hugh hesitated an instant but decided to ignore Smiley. He crawled back on to the roof. He must get down quickly now! He crawled his way laboriously to the other side of the changing-huts, making a disproportionate amount of noise in the process, and then dropped down to the ground where he found himself thankfully hugging the luscious warm greenness.

He lay motionless for some time, looking up through the blades of grass which were so close to his eyes that they were magnified into enormous bright-green stalks. He was fascinated by some ants, and started turning them over with a small twig that he found under his hand. Then he was disturbed by a raucous noise which came from the other side of the building. He managed to get to his feet just before Oscar, Red, Smiley and Don emerged from the lavatory building, laughing and rattling something metallic in their hands. He understood that they had ball bearings. As they approached him, he became aware of a sort of gloating animosity in their attitude to him. He braced himself.

"Luck at that son! 'E gave us three ironies each an' a shillin' as well!" and Don thrust three metal balls forward for Hugh to examine. He scrutinised them, but would not touch. He remained silent and tense.

"Don't count on 's sharin' it with ya, cause yar nat gettin' any of it," said Red triumphantly.

The other four turned to go back to the Puzzle-Walk and there was again talk of the bamboo den. Hugh was surprised that he had got off so lightly, and felt better as he followed them at a short distance. They spoke loudly about the man in the lavatory. But apart from him, they commonly assented that there was little of interest in the park today. They deliberately kept Hugh as an outsider by their loud, boisterous talk punctuated with mischievous whisperings which he knew were directed at him. Then they unpredictably broke into a canter which soon metamorphosed into a wild gallop over the fields. They jostled, pushed and kicked each other, began tumbling, somersaulting, and pulling or swinging on anything that lent itself to their reach. Hugh followed, but still at a distance. As usual in these situations, he just longed for home.

Oscar suddenly spotted two young boys playing with a ball on the grass near the Stranmillis Road gates. They were no more than nine or ten years old, and were kicking a yellow plastic ball. They were well-dressed and obviously from the well-to-do neighbourhood on that side of the park. The four noticed this immediately and the hostility it engendered increased their desire to take a closer look. Oscar was first to reach the unsuspecting youngsters. He bounced stealthily in to intercept the yellow ball as it went from one to the other. Soon the four began to pass the ball between them, sometimes showing it teasingly to the younger boys before whipping it away from them. They played roughly among themselves, trampling the younger boys with undisguised animosity if they got in the way. Hugh looked on, excluded. He was obliged to stand and watch, for he was just as much outside their pleasure as the boys who owned the ball. He felt that he really should head for home, but was frightened that the others might turn upon him and that he would become the next target of their malicious playfulness. The only safe thing to do was to stand fast, witness the scene, and say nothing.

The younger of the two lads began to whimper in a subdued and polite way for his ball. Hugh felt sorry for him. His whimpering soon became more audible when he saw that no one was paying any attention to him. Finally, he sobbed loudly and at length. Red, afraid that they were too near the gates and that someone might come to the rescue, ran up to the boy and thrust the bright yellow ball into his face: "Here's yar ball ya gurny wee bastard!"

The ball struck the other on the nose and a tiny trickle of red began to run on to his upper lip. The boy yelped fiendishly, like a pup whose paw has been trampled on. The older boys distanced themselves from the scene. Hugh was glad it was over.

The group fought and karated its way through the Puzzle-Walk, stopping only at one of the fountains for a drink and a dousing. When they arrived at the gates, instead of keeping straight on down Botanic Avenue, they turned a quick left into the back of Queen's University. Hugh was still some yards behind. Even though he did not want to follow them, he was curious to see what they were up to. He turned left at the gates where, to his horror, stones and insults rained down around him, and it took all his concentration and deftness to avoid the heaviest and most menacing of the missiles.

"Fuck off!" said Red, "We're goin' somewhere."

Hugh, brutally and definitively ejected from the group, turned sullenly away and tramped off. He was hurt; he was smarting all over. It was now abundantly clear to him that he was not, and would never be, part of their gang. Acid tears streamed from his eyes and they cold-burned his hands as he wiped them. He yearned for home, for the shelter from further indignity.

The way back was not short. Every other moment, some threatening event would thrust its jagged way into his consciousness. It was like riding a ghost train and waiting for horror after horror to be thrown in his face. Images of the afternoon came frame after frame into his mind as he passed the low walls of the terraces, and the words "Beast, bloody little animal!" seared and burned their violence on his chest.

At length he reached Shaftesbury Square, and then the dumb and blind street where he lived and which, today, he also received like an insult. He stopped. Still savagely aflame, he looked down the street which was mellowing in the dying orange-glow of sunset. He felt cruelty in the hypnotic blankness of the windows, in the sharp nakedness of the bricks, a cruelty no external light could disguise. He walked swiftly into his house, locking the door behind him. Its quiet engulfed and quickly swallowed him so that his being came to a pause, and he breathed calmly again.

About seven o'clock the next evening, Don called for him to play marbles in the street. There was a timid note of sympathy in his voice as he coaxed Hugh to come out. The latter hesitated, but accepted, and the two were soon standing ready for play at the edge of the kerb. Don held a shiny ball bearing in his hand and was about to throw it when Hugh stopped him.

"It's nat fair if ya play wi' that … I've only ordinary marlies or a couple o' stonies which ya'll break if ya play wi' that."

Don acquiesced, but added that Hugh too could get some ball bearings that evening if he wanted. Then they could both play with them.

"What d' ya mean?" queried Hugh, "Are ya goin' ta see that oul fella tonight?"

"Aye, 'e said e'd be down behind Billy Crone's shap about half-seven. Red an' Oscar won't be there cause they went to a den up the Malone Road this afternoon."

Don stared expectantly at Hugh, waiting on a response.

"Throw down yar marlie," was all that he got.

The afternoon was just falling out of the skies as the boys got into their game. The sun was settling into a liquid golden light which shot up the blackened bricks of the street. They played down one side of the latter and then up the other side, not once going back on their tracks. They played into Stroud Street and then turned left into Wesley Street. When they eventually got to the top of Wesley Street, Don looked across the Donegall Road to the alley which ran behind Billy Crone's grocery shop.

"I bet ya 'e'll be there by nigh … are ya comin'?" he asked. Hugh gathered his marbles and, without a word, began following the other boy towards the alley.

Cut between two tall buildings, the alley was dark and narrow and got very little light. It ran straight ahead for some fifteen to twenty yards, then turned abruptly left behind the row of shops which fronted the Donegall Road. The first of these was Billy Crone's grocery shop. The boys cautiously approached and Don gestured to Hugh to wait a few yards before the turn. From the semi-obscurity of his position, he could hear Don's voice mingle with another in a warm conspiracy. One voice was shrill and light and seemed to flit in and out of the other which was raspy and guttural. Hugh was looking behind him to make sure that no one could see him from the road when Don's voice took him by surprise: "'E says 'e wants you first."

Hugh gave Don his bag of marbles and walked condemned to the corner where he paused. Don encouraged him in a friendly, but challenging way. As he moved on beyond the corner he could just about distinguish, half-hidden in the doorway, a figure in a long grey coat, the upper half of which was leaning backwards against the door. Hugh could not see the face of the man who pressed himself back into the wood. He advanced a little further. Now he could see that the man was grinning, but in a way which made only his top gum visible. The man, who had his hands in his long coat pockets, pulled the unbuttoned coat apart. Hugh could not move.

"Well?" came the rough voice. At the same time, the man grabbed the boy's hand and directed it inside his coat. Hugh's hand was rubbed against the warm, strange flesh which seemed to smell of fish. He pulled his hand away and fled back round the corner.

"I'm nat doin' anymore," he said to Don, "I'm away home."

"No, don't go home … stay at the end o' the entry an' keep nick for 's."

Hugh nodded agreement, and walked quickly round to the front entrance of Billy Crone's shop. The sun had fallen further but was still full on the façade of the building, and sent shafts of coloured light through the shop windows. The upper part of Hugh's body was caught by the slanted beams which gave a ruddy hue to the hallway. He felt exposed by the bloody-warm light, and he drew back for cover. He bent down and began playing unconsciously with bits of rubbish.

When Don came to the hallway, he found Hugh crouching, with eyes almost closed.

"Whad ya doin'?" he asked, surprised.

"Nathin' at all."

"You were supposed ta be keepin' nick!"

"I was."

Don shook his head and then took his hand from his pocket and pushed it forward.

"Ya don't deserve it, but here ya are …" and he dropped a smooth metal globe into the other's outstretched hand. Hugh closed his hand tightly over the big, round object which seemed to deform his clenched fist.

"I'm goin' home," was all he said before crossing the road obliquely to the top of Kensington Street where, once out of Don's sight, he opened his fist to reveal the ball bearing. The last shafts of light picked up the silver and threw it into his eyes so that he had to turn his back on the sun He stared at the ball bearing as if he could not understand what it was, like someone confronted by a familiar object which has lost its original meaning and taken on strange and evil powers.

Hugh walked slowly towards his house. He felt better when he looked up and saw that the sun had finally left the sky. The lines of fine cloud were being pulled thinner by the last throes of light. The sky was shot through with many colours. As he reached the iron grill of the street sewerage, he looked again at the ball-bearing in his hand. He rubbed its smoothness with his thumb and caused its clear surface to smudge.

"It smelt of fish!" he said again to himself, twisting his face in revulsion.

The grill was partly clogged with hardened muck, but he stood vertically above one of the few gaps that existed. He took the silver sphere between index finger and thumb and let it drop. It plunged cleanly between the iron bars and sank—plop!—into the dirty water below. The sound comforted him and caused him to smile sardonically. Hugh lifted his head and gazed down the street's blank succession of openings. Then he turned and walked determinedly towards his house.

The Fight

Thenere was dead bodies in here last time I came up!" said Don, as the three boys rubbed the dirty windowpane with their shirtsleeves in an attempt to see into the room. Oscar and Hugh had not really believed Don when the latter had told them about the existence of the huts and the activities that went on inside them, but their disbelief vanished as soon as they had stood with their hands cupped round their eyes peering into the laboratory. The poorly-lit prefabs, combined with the unwashed windows and the white sheets which were drawn across tables and benches, gave the impression that there was obviously something very sinister going on within. The boys imagined that the results of all sorts of macabre experiments were hidden under the sheets.

The hut they were staring into was one of several belonging to Queen's University Biology Department, and was situated near the side entrance to the Botanic Gardens.

"There was a body on tap o' that table, an' there was bits o' bodies in jars on them shelves!" said Don excitedly. He was naturally given to exaggeration, but the others believed him now because the place was so dark and secretive and had such a sickly-sweet smell of things preserved.

"The students are all on holiday—that's why there's nobody about." Don was evidently well informed as to the comings and goings of those who performed the dreaded experiments he had told them about. Oscar and Hugh were impressed.

The boys moved around the hut searching for a better angle that would reveal exactly what had been going on inside. Unsuccessful, they then tried the door, which was securely locked but which they nevertheless tried hard to push and prise open. Again, no further information could be acquired. After having tried the same procedure on the other huts, they gave up altogether. Don looked round for other sources of interest, but found nothing encouraging near at hand. Frustrated, he suggested that they climb over the railings to the horse chestnut trees along the side of the university.

Chestnuts had been the principal object of their venture on this mild autumn afternoon and, after the parenthesis of the huts, the three were quickly brought back to it. Hugh became worried when he saw the railings because he was a tall, cumbersome boy, who was certainly stronger than the others, but whose strength was insufficient to move his own weight about efficiently. Consequently, he hated climbing. Oscar, on the other hand, was small, light and extraordinarily good at climbing. Hugh was not very keen on Oscar. He especially disliked his face because the latter seemed to have exaggerated features and, in particular, he had exceptionally thick lips. Hugh on the other hand was fine-featured despite the little bit of excess weight which made him appear more baby-faced. They both followed Don who was the smallest of the three. In fact, Don was smaller than anybody else they knew of his age, and he was nicknamed 'the leprechaun'. People said that his growth had been stunted by the fact that he was always smoking butt-ends that he found in the street.

When they arrived at the railings, Oscar was up and over in a flash with something akin to simian agility. Don searched until he found a gap between two distorted bars which he wriggled himself through. Hugh tried to follow but almost got his head stuck. He soon abandoned this and began clumsily to scramble over the railings. They had nasty spikes at the top so he manipulated himself very slowly and carefully until he was able to drop heavily, but safely, to the ground. The other two had not waited for him. He caught up with them at the trees where they were already throwing sticks up at the branches. Hugh realised that they had just stopped talking before he had reached them, and he became intrigued by the unusual silence. He tried not to show his interest, and began scouting around the fallen leaves for a suitable piece of wood. He satisfied himself that they had probably been making fun of his clumsy way of getting over the railings, but he did not really care about that.

When he had found a short but heavy stick, he aimed it at a branch laden with chestnuts. He struck it cleanly, and immediately a cluster of green spiky balls rained down on them.

Hugh was hit on the head by a very large husk which he rushed to open. He cracked it with the stick so that a bitter white sap oozed out. He tucked his fingers into the wound and prised it open to find two enormous shiny-brown chestnuts. He rolled them in the palms of his hands, feeling their smooth shininess and smelling their newly-opened freshness. They were not too tender and would make champion conkers. He put them in his pocket and began eyeing the branches again. As he searched out the chestnuts, he felt someone push him in the back.

"I'll fight ya nigh," said Oscar, thrusting his face forward so that his lips looked even more disproportionate.

Hugh was taken by surprise. Then he realised that this must have been the subject of their conspiracy as he had come upon them. He looked at Don who in turn looked at the ground and was silent. Hugh felt nauseated. He did not want to fight Oscar again. They had already fought twice and Hugh had won both times. The last time was in Kensington Street after a game of football when lots of other boys were around. Hugh had got on top of him; taken him by the ears; and banged his head on the concrete until Oscar yelled in a way that frightened everyone. But Hugh did not like fighting. Other people had pushed him to it and he had agreed reluctantly. Even in victory he was miserable at the thought of having hurt the other boy. Today, the only witness was Don, and this was perhaps his way out.

"I don't wanna fight today," was all that Hugh could muster.

"Yar chicken ..." said Oscar provocatively, knowing instinctively that he would sooner or later get the better of this taller boy. He knew that height had very little to do with winning a fight. It helped of course, but the real stuff came from the inside and you either had it or you had not. Even when Hugh was bashing his head against the ground, Oscar felt Hugh's weakness, he knew that he would one day have the taller boy at his mercy.

"No, I'm not chicken … but I've gadda go home soon for my dinner." Straightaway, Hugh realised how hollow his words sounded, even to himself, and he knew that they would not be accepted. But they were all he had to offer at that moment. The words were met with the contempt they deserved. Oscar's thick lips seemed to have swollen out of all proportion now and as they curved to reveal his sturdy teeth, Hugh was for the first time afraid.

"Admit it, yar scared 'cause ya know I'd bate ya!" came the renewed taunt.

"I don't wanna fight today," was all that Hugh could muster.

"Yar chicken … aren't ya?" and Oscar almost broke into chicken clucks.

"I'll fight ya when ma arm gets bedder next week."

Oscar turned slightly away from him and then lunged forward on to the other boy and they both fell to the grass. They rolled and twisted for several seconds until Oscar wormed his body on top of Hugh's. The latter, to his surprise, did not put up much resistance. His defence was only token because his senses were not really with him. He lay struggling clumsily and half-heartedly against the constantly wriggling quicksilver body of the other. He turned his head sideways into the blades of grass as if to ignore his combatant. He could smell the grass; he could feel it come cold and damp into his back. Oscar was on top, twisting and turning in his wiry agility which Hugh honestly did not feel as a great danger. Hugh gradually relaxed, and lost all trace of fear.

Oscar seemed to want them to turn over and roll in the grass for he was pulling upwards with one side of his body and weighing down with the other. But he could not budge the heavier boy. Hugh lay motionless, locked in the grip he had on Oscar's arms. He was somewhere deadened by the feeling that he was not fully present, that there was only a shadow of him locked in this futile knot. His consciousness was elsewhere. And now, he sincerely wanted to go home: he told himself that he must get home as soon as possible. He could feel his heart pound just as he could feel the beat struggle in the pounding of blood in the hideously thick lips of the other boy. Again he felt sick.

Oscar was so light on top of him! Hugh felt the lack of density in the body that was struggling pitifully to hold him down. He felt as if he could have thrown Oscar high into the air—if he had wanted to. But he did not want to. Even if beaten today, Oscar would be back again tomorrow, and Hugh could not cope with this. This was what made him feel ill. If he wanted the fight to be over soon and to get back home, then he would probably have to help Oscar put an end to it. His back was sinking into the damp leaves and grass and he looked up to see Don's gnome-like face shining like a malevolent green light. He could not go on with this. His arms suddenly broke, and he let go of the restraining grip he had on Oscar. The latter seized upon the opportunity and quickly wriggled his knees on to Hugh's shoulders. He began beating the prostrate body about the face. He landed blow after blow when and where he liked, but he did not really hurt.

Hugh could no longer see nor even feel Oscar. His eyes went beyond into the trees, and again further into the clouds, and still further into the sky. The darkened yellow orangeness of the leaves ran into and out of the white patches hung in blue so that all was a swim of colour. A wind accelerated the swirl so that yellow and orange, white and blue, began to rotate and mix and blur one another. His eyes fixed upon the smudge which was becoming tinted with red.

As he lay staring fixedly into the air, a voice began to seep into him. It was becoming louder—as if coming nearer. Someone was shaking him in an attempt to make him take notice, in an attempt to shake his eyes out of their sockets.

"Do ya give in? Do ya give in? Do ya give in?"

His eyes settled down into his head and he focused unexpectedly upon Oscar's flushed face, upon his fat lips. Oscar's eyes were dilated, large and brown. Hugh still could not hear clearly, and understood the message mainly through lip-reading.

"Do ya give in?" came the relentless questioning once again, desperately urging him to say something.

Hugh had already given in. He could not grasp the point of the question. The voice seemed distant again, as if coming from the end of a long corridor.

"Aye alright, aye … aye, I give in. Leave me alone." This time it was his own voice coming from somewhere far off.

Oscar released his shoulders and sprung to his feet. Hugh rose very slowly, his face bleeding. It was numb, obtuse. But it did not hurt. The wind made the cold in his back come through much sharper into his consciousness. Oscar watched him get to his feet and then brush himself self-consciously. The smaller boy, radiant with the glow of victory, watched how ill at ease the other was. His arm sprung out and pushed Hugh who, taken unawares, almost fell over. Hugh moved dejectedly away from Oscar and Don until he reached the railings again. He refused to go through the ignominy of climbing these once more whilst they were watching, and so instead, made his way out of their sight to a spot where he could take his time. He stood with his back pressed against the cold metal bars. He could hear the others talking appreciatively of the fight which he felt had not taken place. He heard Oscar gloat over the point that he had "bate him fair and square," and Don was obviously in agreement with this judgement, for the leprechaun was giving frantic details about the fury of punches Oscar had unleashed against the bigger boy.

Unexpectedly, Oscar began making fun of Hugh's surname by singing "Oul McDonnell had a farm ..." and accompanying the song with an exaggerated repetition of chicken sounds. But names had never hurt him, even if the song meant that, for the time being at least, he had lost a certain amount of respect, and with it the right to be called by his first name.

After a brief silence, he heard sticks again crash into the branches. He decided to move to a spot where he could no longer see nor hear them. When he had reached Botanic Avenue he found some bushes that completely covered the railings. Here he began his laborious assault, which was all the more difficult given the stiffness he now experienced in his limbs.

When safely on the other side, he walked to the corner where he stopped to look at the two impish figures happily lashing sticks into the trees. Hugh did not look a long time at Oscar. He did not hate the latter; he did not even resent him and he certainly did not fear him. In a way, he perhaps admired his tenacity. At least now he would be left in peace—however ignoble.

His eyes rested upon Don. He and Don had been the best of friends at primary school. One year, they had spent most of their summer holidays together. In almost all cases, Hugh had been the one to protect his friend. This year they had seen less of each other because they had gone to different schools for the first time. Obviously some of their interests had changed, but Hugh had still felt that they would remain friends forever, that there was something unbreakable in the bond between them. He could never have imagined that Don would side with someone else, that for some reason he resented him. Hugh could not understand why the other had remained so silent. In his heart, he began to hate the smaller boy.

Disillusioned, Hugh turned away and began walking nonchalantly home. He put his hands in his pockets and felt the shiny conkers which he stroked appreciatively. His face was cut and still bleeding slightly. He had been beaten and was more than a little ashamed of himself. And who would now believe that he was not afraid of Oscar? At the same time, he did not care. In fact, he felt strangely alive and relieved to be walking along the road in a new sort of freedom.

Initiation

If ya don't watch the friggin' ball, I'll break yar skinny neck!" Angus had again let the ball go past him without attempting to stop it. He hadn't really been looking, and when awakened from his reverie by the screams of his own team, it was too late: the ball was trickling past him into the net. Now Armstrong stood before him with his face contorted, carefully controlling his gestures so that no one else was aware of his threats. He towered over Angus menacingly.

"It's not my fault if I don't like football … you should put somebody else in nets," came the plaintive response.

Angus was frail, with shoulders close to his chin, as if he was always trying to squeeze into an even smaller space than the one he so timidly occupied. He turned to pick up the ball which was just a couple of yards behind him. Armstrong turned in the opposite direction and hurried back to take up position in the middle of the field.

"I don't want to play their silly football," Angus thought aloud, as he tried half-heartedly to kick the ball up to the other boys. Armstrong glared at him from a distance when it failed to come even half the space which separated them.

"I didn't come to camp to stand all day between two sticks trying to stop a ball getting past me … what stupid nonsense!" Angus spoke loudly, with the courage stemming from the unlikelihood of being heard.

It was a beautiful Saturday afternoon, the first day of Scout camp, the first day away from the summer monotony of the street. It was not hot yet, but the sun was warm even though the air was fresh. Angus looked up and was stunned by the deep blue crispness. He dropped his head sharply and became almost dizzy as his eyes were submerged by the varied pools of thick green earth beneath him. He felt extremely annoyed when the cries of the boys shattered the air's thin membrane, and his heart beat faster when he heard their boots thump into the ball. He listened with revulsion as their bodies heaved after it in mindless pursuit. They spoiled the day. Except John. "Where *is* John?" he asked himself, looking down the field, straining to discern John's slight frame.

"Ah, there he is!" John too had joined their band—for the time being. He too was running about like a lost soul. Angus could just about make out the silhouette of the other boy, for he was a bit short-sighted. He distinguished John's wiry frame dimly, but he knew the other so well that his imagination gave him a vivid picture of the expression on John's intense face. He pictured him fighting grimly and doggedly, lost in a maze of arms and legs, his face set firm in determination. John refused to be excluded. Those small, fixed eyes of his would be focused at all times on the ball, and he would see nothing and no one else. He *must* get his kick. Poor John's teeth would be locked and his fists would be clenched as he fought earnestly, if pathetically, for the ball. He could be such a simpleton sometimes.

Angus did not care. It was just one of their differences. His eyes stopped squinting and when the strain of looking disappeared, he relaxed back into the lush patches of high grass behind the playing-field. After all, he was happy to have come to camp with his friend, even if it did mean having to wait for him between two wooden posts while the Owls and the Vultures played the Eagles and the Kestrels. And he was very glad to get away from home.

As his dim eyes delighted in the greenness of the earth, he discerned a little burst of colour to his right. "Flowers!" he exclaimed and moved closer to the patch. Yes, he could clearly see little white and blue buttons gleaming in the sun. On his hands and knees he covered the five yards which separated him from the flowers which were partly concealed by a clump of high grass—evidence that the field was not often used for football. It was an irregular field, bordered on three sides by the tall dark-green trees of Tollymore Forest. The goalposts were in fact branches that had been stripped of ramifications and shoved into the earth, with a rugged crossbar spliced on to them. They cracked in the wind. The forest was mainly pines which stood erect and close together, keeping the sun off a large part of the field. The way the sun struck the trees made parts of them look metallic green, and when they oscillated in the wind, moving blotches reflected the sun as if they were scales. The sun occasionally hit the flowers which were round centimetres of white and blue intensity sown on to very thin pale-green stems that were translucent when Angus held them up to the light. He picked them one by one and held them in the air like trophies. He was happy, but even in the midst of his contentedness, his heart plunged when the cries of the boys pierced his consciousness.

"Beasts!" he said, addressing the trees. His intonation and vocabulary were foreign to normal Sandy Row speech.

He looked round in panic, suddenly aware of danger, expecting Armstrong to fall upon him again. But it was John running up to him.

"Get back in nets Angus!" he cried, trying to catch his breath. "You better do as I say and get back in!" when he came to a halt, he began to pant heavily.

"Your face is all red, John!" said Angus with concern.

"I don't care what ma face is like—you get back in them nets!"

"I don't want to … I don't care, John … I don't want to play." Angus looked down at the flowers in his hand and then bent to harvest some more.

"Armstrong'll kill you if ya let in another goal!" But Angus did not answer. John looked at him closely and noticed an almost imperceptible twitch at the side of his face.

"Oh Angus!" he knew that it was useless to argue any further, so he turned and ran back to the commotion which was presently situated in the middle of the field. Voices were raised in fierce dispute. In spite of himself, Angus looked up and watched the others for a moment. As he sat squatting with his eyes screwed up, a faint feeling of superiority came over him. He was quite happy that he could not see them distinctly, and felt remote and safe and somehow strangely light in the afternoon sunshine.

The noise was coming nearer. They were fighting for the ball about half-way up the right side of the pitch. The noises suggested that they were moving crab-like from one side of the field to the other, but nevertheless getting closer each time. Angus felt an unexpected flush come over him, which he refused to yield to. He sat down in the long grass with his back to the players, picking flowers. Unable to think clearly, he began using his hand as a scythe to swipe at the flowers. They were slowly but surely approaching. He sweated and swiped aggressively at a flower, and a little, blue button bounced over his hand. He could almost hear them breathe now, but he refused to look up. He was startled by a dull thud which he recognised as the ugly leather ball having been kicked very hard. But in which direction? In spite of his resolution, he looked upwards and saw that the ball had been lobbed high into the air against the sun. It continued moving upwards for what seemed like an eternity and his heart followed it into the liquid-blue light. Then it started to come down. Its trajectory took it on an inevitable path towards

Angus's goal. He became aware of a sort of stillness, a pause: why was no one charging after it?

"Angus!" he heard his name fracture the air, and immediately he sprang to his feet and scrambled towards the posts. He was closer than anyone else, so despite his clumsiness, he was sure to get there first. The ball bounced several yards in front of the goal and, having misjudged its course, he almost fell over as he tried to change direction. He also misjudged its speed, for the ball bounced again and began to roll relatively slowly.

"Angus!" he heard them cry again, and his heart quickened. He must get to the ball before it crossed the line—he was almost there. He took a wild swipe at it with his right leg—and missed. With the momentum of his effort he crashed awkwardly into the ground and hurt himself. The ball crossed the line.

He lay on the ground completely inert, his face pressed into the earth and his body stinging with pain. Armstrong was first to get to him and helped him to his feet with what seemed like—from a distance—genuine concern. Angus looked humbly and appealingly into the other boy's eyes which were quietly incandescent with animosity.

"I'm gonna crack yar skull ya wee fart! Ya wee turd!" he said in a forced whisper that only Angus could hear. When Armstrong slackened the hold he had on Angus's arm, the latter almost fell to the ground again. The others soon arrived and Armstrong walked furiously away with the ball

Angus's knees and arms stung and his hip felt dislocated so that he could hardly move. But there was nothing serious: the earth was hard and had scraped him badly, but no bones were broken. John rushed to take Armstrong's place at his side and then Skipper arrived on the scene.

"Alright son?" he enquired with an encouraging smile. He inspected the flesh which was inflamed in patches, and then got Angus to stamp his feet as if he was trying to put out a forest fire. "You bedder take 'im over to the tent, John, an' put some TCP on 'im," and John led him away, supportively.

When they got to the stores tent, John went to the First Aid box and brought out a bottle containing an amber-coloured liquid. He brought it over to Angus who was seated on the ground, just inside the tent. John unscrewed the capsule and the tent began to fill with an obnoxiously sweet odour. He poured some on to a wad of cotton wool and pressed it without hesitation on to Angus's knee.

"Oh … oh … it hurts!" and Angus had to lie flat on his back and grit his teeth in order to cope with the smart.

"Don't be such a baby!" John scolded, but looked him sympathetically in the eyes.

"It's alright for you—you're not the one who's hurt!" and this time it was Angus's voice which was full of reproach.

"You're such a baby," returned John, trying hard to be angry, whilst lifting the other leg delicately for treatment.

"Do you want a piece of wood to bite on?"

"Very funny, clever …" but Angus broke off sharply as the dampened cotton wool was pressed on to the other knee.

"If you think this hurts, you better not let Armstrong get you alone!" Angus had forgotten about *him*. It was better not to think about the big brute. So he lay back and looked up at the roof of the tent where the thought of Armstrong quickly faded as he focused his attention on the shifting patterns of spiky leaves and round forms thrown black on the light-coloured canvas. The thin canvas was pock-marked and dappled dark.

John knelt down beside him. He too soon forgot about Armstrong. He was hoping that Skipper would let them go to town that evening so that they could buy some sweets and cider. He was always ravenous at camp, but more so this afternoon as Angus had cooked for the patrol at lunch time. John still had a vague taste of charcoal in his mouth.

"I'll buy some crisps if he lets us go tonight ..." he was thinking aloud. Angus felt warm and comfortable, with the sting of his wounds subsiding into a sort of pleasant glow.

"I wish it would rain so that we could lie and listen to the drops splash from the branches on to the tent ... I could listen all night to that," he said rhapsodically.

"Don't be so stupid, Angus! We want to go to town," and John was genuinely angry this time. He could not understand his friend's selfishness. It was just like him not to want to do anything. He wondered why Angus had bothered to come to camp in the first place—he could just as easily have stayed moping in his room at home, as he usually did. John thought again of the cider: sometimes his father would give him a little with his food—never very much. At camp he loved to buy cider: it was one of the good things about coming away, and one that he was not about to give up—not even for Angus.

The football match was evidently over, for the din of approaching voices was becoming increasingly louder and had for effect to shake them both out of their daydreaming. They were annoyed and more than a little afraid. The match had finished because the Eagles and Kestrels had gone too far behind to make it worthwhile attempting to catch up, and their players had eventually lost interest in the game. No one, with the notable exception of Armstrong, blamed Angus in any way. The others accepted him without reserve, and the members of his own patrol were quite used to making allowances for him: they felt it was just a bit of hard luck to be lumbered with him, and there was a tacit agreement that the patrol was made up of five, and not six, members. On the whole, it did not affect their overall results because the Eagles had the most talented members of the troop and usually managed to win the major events anyway. And besides that, Angus was always good for a laugh.

John quickly let down the rolled-up doors of the tent, but did not zip them together. Boys were passing on both sides: somebody stumbled over a guy-rope, and somebody else brushed against the canvas of the tent. Their various conversations seemed too loud, and both Angus and John felt that they were intruding. John peeped cautiously out of a small aperture to see them dispersing to their different tents. Hugh, Skates, Muckie and Stevie entered the Eagles' tent.

John began rubbing his earlobe—a habit he had retained from infancy—and moved his head very slightly over to one side.

"We'd better go over to the others," he advised. He waited for another moment, perfectly still, except for the ever-sodelicate rubbing of his ear. Then he lifted the door-flap. "Come on!"

When they had reached their own tent, they were almost knocked over by Muckie who had just charged blindly out through the flaps and straight into them. He was impressively strong and towered over them, and prevented them both from falling backwards by holding on to them until he had steadied himself.

"I was luckin' for you two!" he exclaimed, still clasping them protectively to his breast as if they were in mortal danger. "We're goin' to play a wide game nigh," and his brawny arms continued to enclose them in their sanctuary. Angus looked up at him plaintively:

"I can't play, I'm hurt," came the predictable protest.

"Hugh says everybody is playin' and that includes *you!*" and he promptly lifted Angus off the ground and then plonked him on his feet as if to stress the point: "It doesn't matter if ya can't run … ya can plank yarself somewhere so that it takes up a bit o' their time in findin' ya. Alright?"

But Angus was not alright. "I'm hurt, I said!" and he turned up his scorched flesh for all to examine. "And I can hardly walk!"

"We'll carry ya and stick ya under a bush, an' when they come ya don't have t' put up a fight," Muckie looked at John and both boys smiled simultaneously at the idea of Angus putting up a fight, "ya just hand over yar white band, that's all."

"But what is the point in playing at all if that's all I'm going to do?" He complained half-heartedly, because he knew that was all he ever did anyway.

"I just told ya … ya'll take up their time an' maybe one of us will be able to run home."

Angus was still not going to be convinced, but he had no time to object again as the other patrols were already beginning to emerge from their tents. Hugh, the patrol leader, came out with a bunch of white bands in his hand which he had begun to distribute to the members of his patrol. He handed one to Angus, smiling affectionately as he did so, indicating that he had taken in the conversation.

"Don't worry, ya won't have to defend this wi' yar life," Hugh winked at Angus knowingly.

Everyone gathered in the centre of the field beside the charred remains of a bonfire. The Eagles were to pair off with the Vultures this time: Armstrong would therefore be on the other team. Angus, though worried, thought that this was how things should be. It was safer to have Armstrong as an adversary, for at least you knew where you stood then. Angus could feel the antagonistic presence of the other boy, and when he glanced behind him, he caught sight of Armstrong's well-developed body, and in particular, the well-defined muscular trunk. But he very quickly looked away, without their eyes meeting.

The Eagles and the Vultures were to get away first, so they started moving off towards the forest. The ring of stones surrounding the burnt-out campfire was to be 'home'. It was a difficult base to defend as it was situated at the converging point of the tents, and consequently you could get very close without being detected. The Kestrels and the Owls split into three groups of four, leaving one group to defend the base whilst the other two went out hunting. Armstrong was not a patrol leader, but for games of this kind he was always given the responsibility of a group simply because his physical build imposed such recognition.

Hugh and Muckie took John and Angus deep into the forest and positioned them under suitable cover which was in the middle of a thick clump of bushes and trees with wide-spread low branches. It had been a considerable struggle to get to the middle of their dark enclosure, and both boys felt well protected and at ease. Obscurity, relative inaccessibility, and a few surrounding brambles, afforded them a comfortable illusion of security. Hugh had issued them with instructions: when members of the Owls and Kestrels came close, they were to make as much noise as possible and head directly for home, if they could. If not, they were to surrender their bands. They settled down and began whispering.

"I like it here," said Angus, "it's like a jungle." They looked around admiringly at the thick growth encompassing them and then tried to see through the knots of branches and leaves. The sky was completely blotted out and they could see no hole in the green prickly blanket. John moved forward on all fours until he came to a spot where, by snapping off a few twigs and pulling off some leaves, he managed to make a lookout hole.

"We'll be able to see who's coming," he said, very pleased with himself. Angus watched the back of his neck straining forward. The humidity was beginning to seep into Angus's clothing and he sat up irritably. There was a heavy, stale, moist-green smell trapped in the enclosure with them, and it was beginning to penetrate him so that his irritation increased by the minute. He took a bar of chocolate from the pocket of his shorts and offered it to John who—he had not realised—was still peering through the hole which had a tendency to be enlarged and then reduced by the movement of the bushes in the wind.

"I'm not going to hold my arm out all day, John." The irritation in Angus's voice seemed exaggerated even to himself. John turned round and curtly snapped off a piece of chocolate, and then threw the remains in the direction of Angus with a cursory, "Thanks," which was evidence that he was not willing to pay any attention to his friend's changing moods. The chocolate landed within arm's reach.

"Typical!" but Angus's annoyance was tempered by a feeling of disappointment because, as he gazed at John's back, he was made aware that—for the second time today—he had lost him to the game.

Something was evidently amusing John for he giggled nervously as he moved his head from side to side trying to follow the moving aperture and what was going on beyond it. Angus sighed, defeated. The pleasure in his surroundings had totally vanished now and he felt bored. He picked up a twig and began prodding the soft earth. He felt oppressed and wanted to escape. It was cold now too, especially since his backside was getting thoroughly damp. He tried to get up, but was soon reminded of the pain in his hip, and rolled backwards.

"Sssh!" said John without turning, "I think I saw someone over there," and he motioned with his head as he continued to gaze intently.

"So what? Big deal!" Angus could no longer control his resentment, and made no attempt to whisper. John was flabbergasted. How could he talk like that at this point? When there was no one about, he had been whispering. Now that there was certainly someone, perhaps even someone dangerous, he talked loudly as if it was of no consequence. It seemed that he always willingly invited catastrophe. Why could he not understand this? Why was he always provoking disaster?

John returned to his lookout post just in time to see the outline of someone moving behind the bushes. He felt betrayed and a little sick. Angus watched his back: his fair hair curved on the nape of his neck. He sat crouched, as if the upper part of his body was on a spring about to be released. Angus wanted to touch the back of his neck and ask for forgiveness.

John was just about to start screaming at the top of his voice when he suddenly fell backwards. He had seen Armstrong right in front of them, peering and poking with a stick at the undergrowth. He bent over to Angus's ear. "Armstrong!" he exhaled, at the same time indicating with his finger. They were deathly silent. Angus doubly regretted his outburst of spleen, and his eyes searched John's for reconciliation. But the latter was already formulating a plan of escape. He began miming that he was going to crawl out the back and that Angus must remain where he was, absolutely silent. He hoped to lead the intruders away from their shelter. Stealthily, he began to work his way backwards, going fully down on his belly. He crawled feverishly through the undergrowth, and was torn quite badly by brambles, until he was almost free.

"There's somebody in there!" he heard someone cry, and immediately he writhed himself free and rose to his feet. He made straight for home, screeching his head off as he leapt over a bush and tore through the forest. At the same time, Hugh and Muckie sprang from some trees about fifty yards away to the left of this hiding place, and began running silently towards camp.

Three of the hunters were about to start off in pursuit when they were halted by a yell from Armstrong: "Leave them!" he commanded. The others turned back, looking at him amazed and bewildered.

"One of them's still in here," and he pointed to Angus's hideaway with his stick. "Aren't ya, ya little shite?" he added menacingly, addressing Angus. "Spread around the bushes," he told the others, who did so without question.

Angus sat completely still, his chin pressed into his breast, his small, dim eyes peering at the gap where John had been on the lookout. For a minute there was total silence and he held his breath, wondering what on earth they were up to. His backside was by now very cold and damp, and the muscles in his thigh were beginning to cramp. He turned his head to one side: there was scratching behind him—someone was definitely trying to get in the way John had got out. It was Armstrong. Angus heard him swear under his breath. The big brute was again too close to him. The feeling of nausea was returning, but still he did not move. Armstrong was too big for the opening, but he eventually managed to scramble through until he was close enough to grab the back of Angus's belt which he pulled until he had trailed Angus under him, and then he punched the younger boy in the chest. Angus did not cry, but uttered a muted noise as he curled his body into a painful ball.

"Give me the band!" said Armstrong loudly, for the benefit of the other boys. Angus continued to lie inert on the cold earth, making no gesture of resistance whatsoever. Armstrong punched him again, this time in the gut, and he rolled over squealing. Armstrong twisted the white band and wrenched it from his arm causing the rubber to burn the soft flesh.

"Leave me alone!" came the squealing plea from the prostrate body.

"Give me the band!" Armstrong said again in the same commanding tone that meant he would stand no resistance, and before Angus had time to say anything else, another well aimed blow struck him between the shoulder-blades. As his body flopped over to face the ceiling of branches, he noticed that Armstrong's face was seared by three red lines that streaked his cheek. At that moment, he was lifted to his knees and bundled forward to the opening that John had made and that Armstrong had considerably enlarged. Though he protested vociferously at the rough handling, Angus did not resist physically, and so his frail body was easily trundled through brambles and spiky twigs which tore his clothing. Armstrong pushed relentlessly until both emerged from the natural shelter to where the other three hunters stood waiting. Angus had been beaten. He lay scratched and hurt at the feet of the boys who looked down upon him with a mixture of sympathy and scorn. One of them, a fat and harmless boy called Williams, hastily suggested that they go after another group.

Armstrong's answer was to turn his head slowly round for examination, and Williams looked fascinated at the three pearls of blood that sat at the end of each red score on the cheek.

"The little pig scrabbed me ... he fights like a wee girl!" and Armstrong bent over and picked Angus up by the shirt. "We're goin' to initiate 'im!" he said determinedly.

Angus opened his small eyes wide: for the first time they were filled with terror. He had been almost immune to Armstrong, almost indifferent to the pain and to the constant threat of the other's presence. In fact, in a vague sort of way he was conscious that he was deriving a certain pleasure from Armstrong's endless persecution. But now he was deeply afraid, though still a little incredulous because he could not fully believe that they would initiate him. They had withdrawn from it at the previous summer's camp—which was his first—when, at the very last moment, they had been frightened by his convulsive movements. He had been in such a state that they had decided to leave him alone. Angus saw himself again bound and humiliated, and he began to fret.

"Please leave me alone ... let me go—you've got the band ... leave me alone, please, I got initiated last year." The other boys, apart from Armstrong, were sensitive to his pleading. At the same time, they had not really forgiven him for being the only member of the troop not to have been initiated. They had all been obliged to go through it and had done so, not only without protesting in most cases, but also with a great deal of bravado. It was unfair that Angus had been allowed to escape. Even Angus had felt a certain injustice afterwards, and regretted that he was not a fully-fledged member of the troop.

Suddenly Armstrong thrust his bloody face into Angus's: "We're gonna stake ya out!"

"But I was staked out last year ... please ..." Armstrong grabbed him by the lapels of his shirt:

"Ya bloody little liar! Ya slobbered and slobbered until everybody let ya go but we're nat gonna let ya go this time!" Armstrong let him drop, and then produced four pieces of sisal from his pocket and began to wave them triumphantly in front of Angus who was now pleading pathetically for them to let him go back to camp. His eyes were red and wet, and this was visible proof to the others that he believed in the reality of the ordeal. They too believed in it.

"Let's get 'im away from here," commanded Armstrong, and all four boys seized Angus, Armstrong covering his mouth with one hand.

They carried him for about two to three hundred yards until they came to a narrow, but well-sheltered clearing where they lowered him safely to the ground, while continuing to hold him securely. Fat Williams sat on his chest and giggled whilst another boy replaced Armstrong as Angus's gag. Armstrong went to collect four very sturdy pieces of wood of about ten inches in length which he intended to use as stakes. He had no difficulty in finding these items in the thick woods they had just made their way through, and returned quickly to sink the first two pieces of wood into the earth which gave way easily under the weight of his effort. He then helped the others to begin undressing Angus who was contorting his body in all ways, now and then letting out a muted cry. They pulled him up; stripped him to the waist; and then pushed him back to the ground near the half-buried pieces of wood. Armstrong fastened one of his wrists to the stake and then leapt over him to secure the other. Williams plumped back on to his chest again whilst Armstrong planted the two remaining stakes. He used the aid of a stone to bring all four stakes down to the level he considered just right for the job. When finished, he towered over Angus and looked at the result of his labours with a good deal of satisfaction.

"Right lads, take his begs down!" Angus writhed and fought as if his life depended on it and he surprised the others with his reserves of strength and tenacious resistance. But this only encouraged them to be more ruthless, and they brutalised him as they wrenched off his shorts and pants to leave him vulnerable and exposed. He pulled one thigh across the other in an attempt to hide his nakedness. The struggle went out of his body which rested milky-white against the green, and he lay as if dead. He wept.

They stretched his limp and skinny legs and bound his ankles to the other two stakes. Armstrong leaned over and gagged his mouth with a handkerchief. Angus closed his eyes and lay silently sweating on the patch of lush earth which the sun rayed with intense searching beams. Armstrong stood tall above the staked-out body beneath him. The others looked on, but only half-interested now that the thing was done. It was peculiar how his tears had not touched them as they might have—and certainly they were not intimidated in the way they had been the year before. Perhaps it was because the tears had not been accompanied by any sound, save a few muffled snorts. They looked at Angus's stretched out limbs, and smiled. The body was ridiculously white and incongruous against the deep-green background. The legs were long and looked disjointed and he still persisted in trying to bring one thigh across the other to conceal himself. The ribcage rose and fell as he breathed spasmodically, and the skin was rhythmically pulled tight over the ribs. The flesh looked curiously translucent as a beam from the late afternoon sunshine struck it at an angle. It looked like a milky colloidal suspension someone had carelessly spilled on the grass.

Angus's head was turned sideways and he was still weeping. He avoided the too-bright sky and their jeering eyes. His breathing was halted once again by Armstrong who said quietly, "We're gonna jam ya nigh." Armstrong turned and winked at the others. He nodded to Dee to move a few steps back towards the trees so that he would be out of Angus' line of vision.

"You go an' get the jam Dee," he said out loud, and the latter winked back at him before moving away.

"We're gonna put jam on yar wee dick!" Armstrong had grabbed Angus by the chin and twisted his head round to face him so that he could gloat at the reaction which he had caused in the wet, defeated eyes.

"We're gonna put jam on it, an' then all the bees'll come down for a lick!" Armstrong's eyes glowed in this latest piece of vindictiveness. He knew that his idea was preposterous because, in the first place, he had no intention of going that far—at least not today—and secondly, Dee could not go for jam without the others, and especially Skipper, becoming aware of what was going on. That was the last thing he wanted. His idea also seemed ludicrous to the other three boys present, which is why their compliance and participation was immediate. It was just playful pretence. But to Angus it was real. Armstrong had already gone further than he would have believed.

As they looked at his stretched and strained body, they were jolted from their amusement by a sharp convulsive movement that seemed to be accompanied by noises which suggested that Angus was choking. The handkerchief began to disappear into his mouth. They became frightened and glanced at the spasms of the naked white mass, and then at one another, in stupefaction. They were paralysed. Then, Dee ran from behind a tree and rushed up to Angus to pull the gag from his mouth. When he succeeded in this, they were made even more terrified by the piercing whelping sound that came from his lungs. It was almost supernatural, and accompanied by a rocking of the head and the eyes which shone their whiteness to the sky. Quickly, Armstrong took his knife and cut him free, but the freedom only exaggerated his rapid snapping movements.

"He's gone into convulsions!" said a voice from behind. Armstrong began shaking the prostrate figure violently, but to no avail. Suddenly, he clenched his fist and smashed Angus in the face. The jerking movements stopped. His lungs emitted an acute wailing sound and then were stilled. He rolled over and the others watched the back of his naked body, fascinated. They sighed with relief when they noticed that he was beginning to breathe almost normally again. His ribs opened and collapsed like an accordion, but rhythmically.

"He was only puttin' it on," said Armstrong, unconvincingly. The others did not look at him. At this point, members of the other teams began to arrive. Then Hugh and Muckie, followed by John who was accompanied by Skipper.

"Who staked 'im out?" asked Skipper pugnaciously, rushing up to them and immediately spotting the four pegs in the ground. "Who did it, I said?" and his voice became venomous as he approached Armstrong.

"We all did, Skipper," replied the others, meekly.

"Oh ya did, did ya?" and he turned to face them.

"Skipper, he hadn't bin initiated an' that's all we were doin'," added Armstrong. Skipper had been waiting for Armstrong to say something, and he promptly grabbed him by the shirt and, controlling himself, pushed him slowly and resolutely backwards.

"You're on fatigues for the rest of the camp, Armstrong."

He then turned away from him, to the violated figure lying on the ground, still pressed into the earth. Skipper picked him up and pulled him against his chest. Once hidden from the eyes of the others, Angus sobbed freely. Hugh gave Skipper Angus' shirt which he draped over the bony shoulders with one hand, still supporting the boy with the other.

"Put this on ya, son," he said in a caressing voice, and helped Angus on with his shirt. Angus was then given his underpants which he fumbled a bit with before managing to get them on. He

108

did the same thing with his shorts, anxious to hide his lean, naked thighs. He fumbled ignominiously. He looked somehow indecent to them as he tried to hide himself, and they had to avert their eyes, staring uncomfortably into the forest. Fully clothed, he did not look any more decent, as he stood bent and shaken. He sobbed again, and the others felt injured and, in some strange way, shared his indecency.

"Yar alright lad," said Skipper, putting a hankie to Angus's swollen cheek and looping his thick arm around the boy's head, protectively. John walked beside them as they slowly made for home, whilst Hugh and the others pulled the pegs out of the ground.

Evening came quickly. No one was allowed to go into town. A few boys sat around the campfire until it was time to go to bed, which they did willingly. Back in their tent, the other members of the Eagles patrol were surprised to find Angus in fairly good spirits. He joked as they undressed by torchlight and laughed at the deformed silhouettes thrown against the canvas. When their torches were extinguished, and they were all quiet, they could see the dancing shadow-game on the canvas of the Vultures' tent, from which there also issued some loud laughter, which Skipper was quick to dampen.

Angus lay contentedly, looking up at the roof of the tent. He felt satisfied, despite the utter exhaustion that charged his body and the distant pain which told him that somewhere he had been mortally wounded. But he put those feelings aside and experienced a wave of pleasure which forced him to smile to himself. He became strangely elated. Out of some nebulous depth came to him the realisation that the source of his elation lay in the knowledge that he had been initiated. He was no longer an outsider. He was part of the patrol, a member of the troop, at one with the others now breathing quietly at his side. He raised his body quietly to check that Hugh, Muckie, Skates and Stevie were already asleep. Then he turned to John and moved closer. John had been expecting him. Angus nestled his head into the other's sleeping-bag. He need no longer be afraid. But he was never afraid anyway when he nestled cosily into the soft down of John's sleeping-bag.

Plunder

What th' fuck did we come to th' gardies today for?" said Red, taking time out from meticulously etching his initials into the wooden bench of the bandstand to look quizzically at Oscar.

"Wasn't my fuckin' idea!" replied the latter.

"Wasn't mine either," said Hugh.

"Nobody ast you … you just follied 's," contributed Smiley, with an antagonistic and accusatory edge to his tone which created a brief silence. Red looked at Hugh to see if he was going to react to the implied challenge but the boy just looked vaguely into the air, feigning disinterest.

"We better check out a few dens on th' way back … w' need some dough." Red had reached the awkward age of seventeen. His body was shaping into that of a young man's but it seemed to be an effort for him to move it from one place to another. He had long, bushy red sideburns which he razored into sharp, oblique lines that cut into his cheeks. On the front of his chin there was some sparse, ginger stubble. He jerked his body forward in a clumsy movement which was the signal to the others that they were to head for home.

Oscar, always quick to notice the slightest change within his field of vision, suddenly exclaimed: "There's Helen!"

Red stopped, turned round abruptly to follow the other boy's look. He smiled to himself, it was her alright, the silhouette was unmistakable.

"Bet ye sh's nat wearin' any knickers!" said Oscar.

"Let's see if sh' is," said Red, and the four boys moved off in the direction of the rose garden where the outline of the young girl could be seen zigzagging randomly in and out of the colourful beds of flowers. Hugh maintained a slight distance behind the others: he had a feeling that something was likely to happen that he didn't really want to be part of. But neither did he want to be excluded—another exclusion would be final.

Oscar attracted the girl's attention with a two-fingered wolf whistle. She stopped abruptly and waited for them to come closer.

"Hello Davey!" she said, looking at Red. This surprised Hugh, but he quickly caught on when she then addressed Oscar as 'Johnny'. Both boys eagerly returned the greeting and then Red quickly introduced Smiley as 'Billy' and Hugh as 'Tommy'.

"Pleased to meet you," said Helen, looking at Hugh in a way that made him feel uncomfortable. He registered that her accent was not like theirs, not from the streets around Sandy Row.

"Whadya doin' this afternoon, Helen?"

"I just thought I would go for a walk among the roses since the weather is so nice. Would you like to come with me?"

"All of us?"

"Yes, why not?"

"Aye, okay, if that's what ye want."

The group meandered its way through the stunning array of brilliantly deep colours and heavy perfumes. Red suddenly moved closer to the girl and slipped his arm around her waist. Oscar looked slyly at Smiley, closing his fist and making an easily understood gesture by moving it rapidly back and forth.

The couple in front of them began whispering together as if conspiring in some very secretive plot. Red's hand slipped on to the girl's backside. He turned to the others. "Helen says she wants 's to go back to her house with 'er. Whadya say?"

"Aye certainly!" said Oscar, eagerly accepting the invitation with a glance at Red's hand and then a wink at him.

The group now walked with more intention towards the park gates which they soon went through, continuing up the terraced street towards the Stranmillis Road. They crossed this road and walked for another five minutes before coming to a halt outside a large, gardened house. Hugh felt uneasy, intimidated. He wished he had stayed in the street and not followed the others this afternoon. He didn't want to go inside the house but after opening the front door and ushering the boys inside, Helen stood looking at him strangely.

"Aren't you going to come in Tommy?" She pulled the door back further in invitation.

Hugh winced at hearing her use this name. He felt ill. He couldn't even decide whether or not he liked her. He certainly didn't find her attractive: her lips were too full and too thick; her skin too freckled. And there was something repulsive about the eyes which tried too hard to pierce the inside of him. Or of anyone for that matter. She looked insistently at him.

"Come on … I won't bite you."

He could hear raucous laughter already coming from inside the house. Red suddenly called out his name—his new name. On hearing it, he brushed past the strange girl who, with a serpentine movement of the body, managed to touch him with her hip. She then locked them in.

On entering the room, Hugh saw Red seated in a wide armchair, his right leg draped negligently over the side. He beckoned the younger boy to come over.

"You watch the front door, okay?" he said quietly. More audibly he said to the others, "I'm first jockey." He then stood up and walked towards Helen who was standing in the sitting room doorway. He dropped his hand between her legs and nodded with his head to the stairs.

"I'm second," said Oscar to Smiley.

"I'm third," said Smiley looking over to Hugh and completing the pecking order. The latter gave no response but began looking fixedly from behind the bow window curtain into the garden. He listened to the light footsteps of Red and Helen as they climbed the stairs to the girl's bedroom.

Oscar set about opening and closing dresser drawers; displacing objects; turning over cushions and seats; scrutinizing the contents of boxes and whatever divers containers he could lay his hands on.

"Nat much in here," he looked disappointedly at Smiley.

"Let's try the kitchen. Anyway, I'm fuckin' starvin'."

Hugh continued to gaze out the window, seemingly absorbed in his allocated duty. He was frightened the girl's father would turn up unexpectedly. After a few minutes, he heard Oscar come back into the room. He turned to look and saw the other boy holding a half-eaten chicken leg and a salt cellar.

"Ye want some? There's plenty in there ..." indicating the direction of the kitchen with a backward flick of the head.

Before he could answer, they both heard the heavy steps of Red coming down the stairs. As he got to the doorway, he fastened first his belt and then methodically did up his flies. When he had finished, Oscar handed over the chicken and salt to him.

"My turn ..."

Red eagerly tore a piece out of the chicken leg with his teeth. He quickly scanned the visual evidence that the room had been given a going over.

"Ye fin' any plunder?" he asked Hugh.

"Ask Smiley ... I was keepin' nick."

Red walked lightly towards the kitchen which he found empty, and then into the dining-room where he caught Smiley slyly slipping something into his pocket.

"What's that ye gat?"

Smiley was a bit startled but disguised his surprise. He reluctantly withdrew a silver cigarette-case from the front pocket of his jeans and obediently handed it over to the older boy.

Red scrutinized it for a few seconds. "Marty's da might buy that … if nat, we'll pawn it. What else did ya fin'?"

"Nathin' else so far … we were just eatin' stuff from the fridge".

Red looked at him suspiciously and then went back into the kitchen where he began rattling the various metal containers that were perched on the different shelves. From the top shelf, one revealed that it had coins inside; Red quickly removed these, counted them, then pocketed them.

"Hi much?" asked Smiley, attracted to the scene by the noise of rattling coins.

"Nat much," came the laconic reply. Red looked at him in a way that let the other know he would not produce the money for his inspection. "A couple o' shillins," he added.

Oscar was heard trudging down the stairs. Smiley looked knowingly at Red. "Me nigh."

Oscar was still demonstratively arranging his clothing when he arrived in the kitchen. "Fuckin' big tits on 'er!" he said appreciatively.

Red made no reply. He was still engrossed in a methodical inspection of the kitchen. The tally was disappointing so far. "There must be a few more bob aroun'," he said, talking to himself and taking no notice of the presence of his companion. His eyes scanned the cupboards and shelves meticulously seeking further clues.

Hugh had been immobile for some time, lodged between the curtain and the wall from where he could get a good angle on the path to the gate. His activity helped him not to think about what was going on within. His immobility was suddenly disturbed by the whistling of Smiley coming noisily down the stairs. He pretended not to hear when the latter came up behind him saying "Your turn."

Getting no response to this, he grabbed Hugh by the arm.

"Ye chicken? "

"No"

"So what's the problem?"

"I don't fancy her."

"Ya don't fancy her!" Smiley dismissed the words with a guffaw of ridicule. "Ye don't luck at the chimney when yer pokin' th' fire son!"

Hugh made no response. He felt confused. It wasn't quite true that he didn't find the girl attractive. He found her strangely attractive but couldn't understand the reason for this, especially when he thought of the traits of her face. Maybe he just wanted to talk to her. He certainly didn't want to do what the others had done. He had not done it before and didn't want it to be with her, not here, not with the others around. Only Red knew he hadn't done it before. Perhaps he would do better to do it now and get over with it, but somehow, he didn't want to 'share' her with them. For some reason he felt angry at the girl. Just then, he heard her call from the bedroom:

"Are you coming up Tommy?"

"Away on up … *Tommy!* Ach, it'll do ye good … 'n' she can't get enough of it …"

"You keep nick then."

"Aye, certainly."

Hugh began mounting the stairs, guided towards her bedroom by her softly singing voice which seemed to encourage him. When he reached her door he could see that she was lying on her single divan, naked from the waist down, her blouse and bra pulled up to her neck. She lay with her back to him, her long, black hair flowing in curls and waves on the white of the pillow. He made an involuntary noise in his throat and she swung her body round quickly to uncover her sex. Hugh froze, captivated by his first vision of a girl's dark and thick pubic hair.

"Come and sit over here," she beckoned him towards the bed. For the first time he gazed deeply into her eyes and was again mesmerized. But what he saw frightened him and made him recoil. There was something horribly wrong in those eyes which held him in a half-mocking, yet enticing, twist.

"You can't leave the room until you give me something …" she said, pulling one knee slightly upwards and outwards, revealing herself further.

"I don't want to give you anything," he said apologetically. "I'm sorry, but I just want to go home."

Helen looked at him determinedly, her eyes dilating to suck him into them.

"Come on," she pleaded, and gestured once more for him to approach. At this point they heard a clattering sound from downstairs as if someone had dropped a drawer or some heavy piece of wood. The distraction was enough to save him from the spell of her eyes and he managed to look away.

"No. I'll see you in the gardies some time." Before she could say anything else, Hugh was out of the room and on his way relievedly down the stairs.

On reaching the bottom of the stairs, Hugh was joined by the others who had finished their rummaging of the lower part of the house and were ready to be on their way. On seeing them, Hugh pretended to fix his shirt tidily into his trousers.

"We foun' a fiver!" said Smiley.

"Let's go," said Red, looking at Hugh knowingly and then pushing him out through the front door and on to the garden path to the gate. Oscar was last, pulling the door quietly to him until he heard the lock click.

"D'ya think it was a good idea t' take th' money?" Hugh looked quizzically at Red as they made their way down the Stranmillis Road.

"Sh's nat goin' t' say anything, is she? Hi's sh' goin' t' explain t' her da that sh' had four boys roun' t' 'er house? D'ya think she'll tell 'im sh' bucked the four of 's? Na, she won't say anything."

Hugh was partly convinced by these words. But mainly, he reassured himself with the thought that, in any event, he hadn't done anything. He wouldn't get a share of the money—they wouldn't share it with someone who still hadn't really proved that he was one of them. Anybody could keep nick. Besides, he hadn't touched her and he hadn't eaten any of the chicken. As he walked on, locked in his own thoughts, a sudden vision of her pubic hair flashed across his mind and caused him to panic slightly. It fascinated him and held him for a moment, but he successfully managed to extricate it from his thoughts. Anyway, Red was certainly right, she probably would never say anything.

The Scarf

It was very cold, as well as being now very dark. In fact it had been getting dark since half-past five, which was almost two hours ago. Hugh stood, impatient, in the unlit hallway of a confectionery shop in Bradbury Place while the lights of the town came forward into the night, pushed forward by the intense darkness. The white road-lighting pierced the obscurity with brilliant and naked shafts, while the orange-yellow coming from numerous shopfronts poured into and warmed the otherwise cold white light. It began to drizzle, and the falling spits caught and broke the bands of light and dark, wrapping the avenue within a series of veils. Hugh was glad to be in the shelter of the hallway, but his happiness became jaded when he thought of his flimsy jacket which did not even protect him from the wind. It was his favourite jacket. He had decided not to wear anything on top because it would not have looked good, and so he had been prepared to get a little bit wet. But as he stood looking out at the fine drizzle, he began to regret his decision.

He had been waiting for more than twenty minutes, and his eyes were beginning to strain under the opaque glare of the neon lights. Each time a bus approached, he would look up hopefully and search out Edna's frail silhouette. It was the period when the peak traffic was just subsiding, but there were still numerous buses passing in both directions. For the time being, each one had been a disappointment despite the fact that every alighting passenger roused his curiosity in one way or another, as he sought consolation in the strange, wan faces gliding past. When the bus had departed, his eyes recovered slowly from the violently illuminated darkness, and he retracted into his almost cosy refuge.

When she finally stepped off the bus, he watched her without moving forward from his den. Edna, like Hugh, was fourteen and although she was lightly-built, she had a curiously lazy heaviness in her feet which she tended to drag as she came towards the shaded shop entrance. Her features were fine, almost to the point of sharpness, and her hair was cut short like a boy's. Her hair, along with the well-defined traits of her lips, nose and eyes, made her look elfish. The elfishness which accompanied her was destroyed only by the lacadasical sweep of the feet, which always irritated him. As she walked towards him, she raised her collar to the wind and drizzle. When she reached him, he put his arm around her and she shivered up against him. She was quite small, and he rested his chin on her head for a moment. Then their lips touched lightly. He was surprised that her lips were so cold and wet.

"Bet ya thought I was never comin'!" she said jovially, raising her dark eyebrows.

"Well, ya did say t' meet ya at seven," he replied playfully, looking down at his watch. He was not going to mention that he also had been a few minutes late.

"Mammy said I had t' do the ironin' or else I wasn't allowed out," Edna made an effort to accentuate her words when she spoke to him because she thought that he spoke better than her. But it only made her language seem self-conscious and unnatural. He was aware of her feeling of inferiority and knew that he had at one point contributed to it by correcting something she had said. He wished now that he had never done so. At the same time, he was partly glad that she was making an effort for him.

"Did she say anything to ya about comin' down the Row?"

"No, sh' just said I had to be in before half-ten. She doesn't mind when I come down ta see ya, although sh' said that you could come up t' the house a bit more often," the latter was both a reproach and a hopeful invitation. Hugh hated going to her house. Edna was the eldest of the family and there were six younger children. The mother was kind, but had great difficulty in keeping abreast of all the things that had to be done, and consequently, many things went neglected. She was negligent in her dress and in her carriage; she was chatty and familiar and possessed a propensity for putting people at ease—which had exactly the opposite effect on Hugh. When he looked at the mother, he felt that she was responsible for the curious laziness in her daughter's walk. He told himself that he was probably wrong to think such a thing, and that he was certainly wrong to recoil from Edna's home. He didn't think that it was snobbishness, but he could not otherwise understand the forces which were at work inside him, placing barriers between himself and others and pulling him inextricably away from Edna.

"Maybe I'll come up on Saturday—if we don't go to the pictures," he said, rather hesitantly.

Edna and Hugh had been seeing one another for about four months. They had met at a birthday party for a girl who lived not far from Hugh in City Street, on the other side of Sandy Row, and who went to Kelvin secondary school with Edna. Hugh had been at primary school with this girl, but lost contact with her when he started going to the grammar school. Edna and Hugh went regularly to parties together, but opted out of most of the games, which meant that they were teased by the others with playful taunts of 'real love' and 'married life'. In a way, they were both flattered by this adolescent talk, although Hugh's deeper feelings were much more ambiguous and complex. Secretly, he was ashamed of Edna, but he would never admit it—neither to her nor to himself. When he decided that he had no right to feel this way, then he loved her and there was teenage passion and complete complicity between them. But, more often, when his ideas about himself and his future took precedence over everything else, then he would push her away, keep her at a distance by making her the victim of his own internal turmoil and aspirations.

They stood holding one another in silence. The drizzle had almost stopped. There were fewer buses, and the marks they made on the road remained longer. Hugh held her closely to him and they both stood for some time with their eyes closed. They kissed again, but more self-consciously than before. Hugh opened his eyes to free himself from a distant feeling of guilt.

"Shall we go for a bit of a walk?" he asked her, and without replying she turned away from him so that he felt again the bite of the wind. He quickly buttoned his jacket and pulled it tight across the front, and then carefully wound his scarf twice around his neck, tucking both ends into the back of his collar.

At the beginning, they simply walked side by side without touching until, stopping in the orange flood of a shop window, he put his arm around her. They walked on together, daringly, but without confidence, stopping now and again to look at records and stereo-sets and, less often, clothes. They walked on through the relative brightness of Bradbury Place and into the quieter and darker University Road, until they reached the silence and obscurity of the streets surrounding the university itself.

As they came up to the older red-brick buildings, it began to rain again, this time more heavily. They decided to go down University Street and look for shelter in one of the generous Georgian doorways. They soon found one that was obviously the entrance to an uninhabited building, for the paint was in scales and part of the fanlight above the door had its windows missing. The rain became heavier still and formed an inch or so of plashing water on the road, and further obscured the red-brick building opposite.

The doorway provided more than adequate protection from the rain which was thankfully being blown away from them. Hugh stood with his back to the still-substantial wooden door and held the girl into his breast. His arms protected her back. They again kissed softly. Something prevented his kisses from becoming intense. Edna was full of warmth and impatience, but he could not respond. He accepted her sentient openness, but he could not return it. As they stood in the dark and cold they felt close, but separate. He was afraid of his feelings for her, and as he hung his head on her shoulder, he gripped her tightly as if he wanted to hurt her. Becoming conscious of the sweetly-pleasant perfume rising from her coat or from her neck, he suddenly released her.

"I'm cold Hugh ... an' my han's are freezin'," she said, rubbing her hands together and blowing into them. Her voice surprised him, as it was distant and sounded rather complaining. He immediately undid the buttons of his jacket and she passed her hands under his arms. They were icy, but he squeezed them into his sides, and she looked up at him thankfully. When they kissed again, it occurred to him that his own hands were also very cold. He told her so. She hesitated, but then undid her coat so that he could slip his hands guiltily into the warmth. A thought flashed through his mind and held his hands immobile for an instant, but he quickly dismissed it and moved his hands deliberately on to the sides of her breasts. She lifted her mouth to him, and this time he took it without hesitation. He moved his head from side to side until he was almost dizzy, and then passed his right hand on to her left breast. She removed his hand without breaking off the kiss, but he pretended not to notice, and worked his hand back again on to her breast. This time she did not remove it, but instead kissed him more feverishly. Her breast was fully rounded, neither large nor small, hard and perfect. He pressed deeply into her, so that they felt joined to one another.

They were unaware of how long they stood there in the doorway, but then the rain stopped abruptly and they momentarily suspended their holding of one another, listening for confirmation. Edna unexpectedly broke the silence by asking him the time. He was reluctant to look at his watch because it meant being ejected from their shelter into the cold and damp reality of the night. But when he did finally manage to make out the hands of his watch, he was seized by a wave of panic when he realised that it was almost nine-thirty. They would have to walk briskly back to Bradbury Place if she was to catch a bus that would take her home before half-past ten.

They moved apart and fastened their coats. Hugh noticed that she was shivering at the contact with the night, so he took his scarf and gallantly wrapped it around her neck:

"You can take it as you have further to go than me." Edna felt privileged as she wrapped the red and white cloth around her. It was his Manchester United football scarf and she knew that it was something he never parted with. She looked up at him and smiled with the side of her mouth only, in recognition.

They smartly retraced their steps, fixed to one another by the hips. He tried to avoid the puddles of water on the pavement but eventually put his foot into the middle of one and splashed them both. His shoes, like his jacket, did not afford protection against the rain, and the water inevitably seeped through to his foot. He did not say anything, but Edna could sense that he was annoyed with himself once more.

As they reached Bradbury Place, they saw a bus approaching Shaftesbury Square. They hurried to the bus stop and got there just in time. Edna jumped on board without their having time to kiss or exchange goodbyes. She sat down and waved to him as the bus pulled away from the stop. When the bus had disappeared from view, Hugh became more acutely aware of the wetness in his shoe and he was seized with a feeling of regret. *I must be daft!* he said to himself bitterly. But as he turned to walk towards Shaftesbury Square, he remembered the perfect firmness of her breast and the unfamiliar touch and smell of her female clothing. He almost smiled, but the nascent smile turned into a sneer at himself. *It just won't do … I shall have to break it off,* he resolved.

No longer conscious of the night, the lights, or even the rare passer-by, Hugh walked across the road, past Mosie Hunter's pub, and then crossed the Donegall Road into Kensington Street. His heart had fallen into his wet shoes. His life seemed to have sunk below his knees and he walked heavily, squelching images of the night, of her round breast, of shop lights and buses, pressing them down into the wet pavement and feeling as if, somehow, he was trying to push himself into the ground.

The next day was Friday and he decided to wait for Edna on her way home from school. Hugh stood at the junction of Sandy Row and the Donegall Road. He was anxious, but determined. *I have to break it off with her ... there's no other way,* he repeated, convincing himself as to the futility of their going on together.

He foresaw a problem in that she would not be alone, and this would mean that he would embarrass her by taking her aside. He regretted this, but then, it just had to be done. *I don't get that much out of it anyway,* he reassured himself. It was almost four o'clock—the time Edna usually came sauntering down the road. The afternoon was full of the noise of traffic, of the bustle of people on the pavements, and the exchange of money and goods in the shops. Edna, since she had met Hugh, had always taken the same route home even though it meant walking a bit further, past Kensington Street, to get her bus. She saw Hugh before he saw her and discreetly arranged her school uniform and ran her hand through her hair before reaching the traffic lights on Sandy Row.

Hugh was still in full discussion with himself. *It's not as if I really loved her—because I don't ... I know she's nice looking ...* Hugh looked up and saw a stream of black blazers pouring over the road at the traffic lights. He saw her approach. She was with her best friend Flo. When their eyes met, she smiled, a smile he in part returned. *I'll have to be nice and calm and try not to hurt her ... there's no reason why we can't still be good friends.*

Edna chatted loudly with her friend. She did not wonder why he was standing there propped against the wall, immobile, looking so grave in contrast to the light-hearted atmosphere and activity of Friday afternoon. She wanted to swing on his arm and pull his hair. For a moment, he thought that it would be better

129

to put the whole thing off, but the sound of her voice brought back his resolution.

"An' what do I owe this occasion to, yar lordship? It's nat everyday I'm granted an audience," she said playfully, waltzing up to him. Hugh smiled in spite of himself, but came closer to her so that her friend Florence would not hear.

"I want to talk to you alone," he said, ominously.

The girl's instincts were immediately aroused. It seemed that somewhere in her consciousness she had always been fearful, and now her wariness sharpened until she was expectant and ready for the worst. She turned to her friend. "You go on … I'll meet ya at the bus stop, okay?" Florence nodded her acquiescence solemnly. Her resentment at being left out was drowned by a sense of drama which was communicated by the silence of the other two.

They watched her advance towards Shaftesbury Square and when she had reached a comfortable distance, Hugh shuffled his feet and turned to Edna, slowly grouping his words together into a sentence, "Edna, I … I …"

But the girl was sensitive to his hesitation and was keen to spare them both any embarrassment. She anticipated what he was going to say:

"I know what yar gonna say," she interrupted, "ya don't have t' tell me … I've bin expectin' it," she looked at him with eyes already clouding over.

"How do you mean?"

"You don't wanna see me again, do ya?"

The simplicity and directness of the question left Hugh without an answer. On all the occasions he had turned the situation over in his mind he had never foreseen this perspicacity on her part. He could never have hoped for such acceptance and fatality which he thought he could recognise in her voice. It was going to be a lot easier than he had anticipated.

"It's alright," she said, trying to cover her wounds by summoning her pride, "there's no point in sayin' anything else." He was amazed that her voice was neither bitter nor aggressive, but simply passive, as if she was bending to forces that were beyond her. She was ready to settle for another place in the scheme of things, and would raise no outward objection. Inside she was hurt beyond expression.

After a moment's hesitation, Hugh stepped backwards and was about to say that he wished they could remain good friends, when Edna once more cut him short:

"I'll bring yar scarf down tamarra … I'll give it t' somebody in th' street t' give it to ya, if that's alright."

"I wasn't going to say that," he protested mildly, then added, "You can keep the scarf."

She looked him straight in the eyes, with a look full of humility and love. The tears which had been swelling at the corners of her eyes began to run gently downwards. She summoned enough courage to say:

"I don't want it, but thanks anyway. See ya …" She turned and walked on along the Donegall Road and round the corner to her bus stop.

Hugh was sorry. He felt ashamed at the thought of Edna having to tell her friend what had happened. He thought too of her parents and especially of her father who would mock her when he would discover that she was not going out at the weekend. He was indeed sorry. He watched Edna until she disappeared out of sight, then looked right at the cars and waited patiently to cross the road. He was thankful that she had let him off the hook.

The next morning he rose late and dressed hurriedly in order to play football with the Crawfords in Stroud Street. They played every Saturday morning, as they were much older than Hugh and worked during the week. Saturday morning was always full of excitement in the street and this morning he was particularly relieved at the thought of not seeing Edna that evening, at being free to do whatever he wanted with his time. After all, it was a burden for him to go for walks in public, to queue up at the pictures and then to fumble with his money at the ticket office. Tonight he would sit at home and watch the television, and this idea pleased him enormously.

He was not surprised to be in such good spirits. The Crawfords played roughly and made little concession to the fact that they were men playing with boys. Hugh always got hurt when he played with them because he insisted on getting his share of the ball, of playing a full part in the game. This morning he was especially energetic and gave himself completely to the match, absolving himself of all other thought whatsoever.

Time passed in mindless activity and total happiness until the last goal was scored and they decided to break up for lunch. Hugh left the others reluctantly. On reaching his home, his mother told him that his friend, Martin Brown, had called.

"He says he'll be back later, an' he left you your scarf," she pointed to the red and white scarf draped over the settee. "He says somebody gave it to him to give to you," and she looked at her son with a faint but knowing smile.

"Where's my dinner, mammy?" he asked, feigning disinterest, and not paying attention to her smile. When she turned away from him, he leaned over to the settee to pick up the scarf.

"Your dinner's out there in the scullery waitin' for you … an' it's just as well it's a salad," she added curtly.

Hugh held the scarf tightly in his hand, partially concealing it as he walked with it into the kitchen. He was alone to eat. His mother seldom ate more than a sandwich or a piece of cake at lunchtime and it was too early yet for his sisters to call in from their shopping. He placed the scarf on the table and began to eat absent-mindedly, his eyes floating unseeingly before him as he drifted into reverie. The scarf had brought with it an uncustomary atmosphere into the house. He had barely thought of Edna that morning, except to conclude that he was sorry, but that she was now already part of his past. The scarf lay on the table beside his plate as a reminder of things hastily forgotten. He went on eating without tasting his food.

In the midst of his daydreaming, he was arrested by an unusual smell coming from his right. Aroused, he focused his attention. The smell was unmistakably coming from the scarf. It was a close, perfumed smell which seemed to rise up and derange his senses. His impulse was to put it away from him, but as he took it in his right hand, he released the odour further and it caught and enveloped him. Looking around to verify that his mother was out of the way, he plunged his face into the scarf. "It smells of Edna," came the quiet recognition. He followed the length of the scarf with his nose, sniffing out the smell until he found the place where it was most intense—the area where the girl had wrapped it round her neck. Hugh was transported on the scarf's perfume, which issued from the cotton and circled his senses until his head turned and he was gone in a sort of delirium. The effect brought him close to tears.

The thought crossed his mind that she may have done it on purpose, that she may have sprinkled perfume on the scarf before returning it. But he quickly rejected this idea—Edna was not a girl who would play games. Trembling, clutching the scarf to his face, he indulged in the sweet, translucent odours which made the objects in the kitchen multiply themselves miraculously. His dizziness was coupled with a feeling of irretrievable loss.

"I was stupid to break off with her!" he said, rising from the chair and then leaning back against the wall. He hid himself from his mother. No one would know how foolish and selfish he had been, how he had made the girl suffer or how much suffering he endured at this moment. He pushed himself against the wall as if he wanted to make himself disappear, at the same time burying his face still further into the sweet-scented scarf. He held the scarf in his mouth in order to prevent any sound from coming out.

When he had stopped trembling, and his mind had once more regained its lucidity, he pulled the scarf from his face and held it open in front of him, like an offering to some strange god. If Edna only knew what revenge it had taken for her! But then, she was someone who would not triumph in revenge. Hugh felt relieved and reassured that his calm had been fully restored now. He looked at the red and white scarf as a bringer of some greater truth.

The Match

Linfield was playing Distillery at Windsor Park. Hugh had always been a keen Blues supporter but had stopped going to the matches because he was getting to an age when it became embarrassing to ask a man to lift him over the turnstile. He was now a tall, slender fifteen year-old and awkward in his bigness. From the queues of supporters on Saturday afternoons, men would look at him with a knowing smile when he would make his humble appeal of "Would ya lift is over, mister?" In the past year he had been getting more and more refusals and sometimes he was just lucky enough to get into the stand after the start of the game. He refused to spend the little pocket money he received on going to football matches, preferring instead to earmark the money for pursuits other than the dubious pleasure of watching Linfield.

It was a Tuesday evening Cup game and Hugh watched the crowds stream up the Donegall Road, the pavements awash with red-white-and-blue scarves and bonnets. Football supporters always walked fast going to a match, their desires and anticipations translated into the speed which sometimes caused people to collide at the entrances to shops or at bus stops. Hugh looked at the faces of the men rushing by: they were all lit up by the same childish energy and excitement at being out in the road, leaving behind their mundane obligations. Wave after wave rolled on until the last major undulation spilled across the traffic lights. It was a seven-thirty kick-off, and by seven o'clock there were barely only one or two red-white-and-blue caps left, bobbing up and down the parallel pavements stretching to the library bridge on the other side of Sandy Row. The excitement was contagious, and Hugh would have liked to have gone to the match. As he watched the stragglers from the top of Kensington Street, his feeling of agitation was turning to disappointment and an acute sense of abandonment. The light of day was fading along with his excitement, both synchronised with the disappearance of the eager football supporters.

Hugh turned his back on the Donegall Road and walked dejectedly to his house which was only a few doors from the top of the street. He went to the parlour where he reluctantly took his schoolbag and began his homework for the next day. He first tried to do his maths. It is difficult to say exactly when maths had become a foreign language to him, spoken by people who had no connection with his age or his street. He could solve 'problems', but he had no interest in what had become to him a latinised form of abstraction—a dead foreign language. After some time pondering fruitlessly and disinterestedly over his books, he decided that the best solution would be to wait until he got the answers from fatty Moore the next morning on the bus. He closed the book and pushed it back into his army-type schoolbag, at the same time extracting his *Faber Book of Modern Verse*.

They had been studying a poem in class that day and he had to learn a verse for the first period next morning. He liked poetry. Strange how it seemed to be at once foreign and unfamiliar and yet rhymed to a beat which was in harmony with an internal rhythm. If the lines were spoken out loud they sounded discordant or simply laughable. He could sympathise with people who considered that boys who liked poetry were effeminate. He went to a single-sex school, and when he heard classmates recite poems he often felt that way too. It was the unnaturalness of the voice that they put on. Poems had to be said internally; spoken, but voiceless. The verse he had to commit to memory was the last verse of Mathew Arnold's 'Dover Beach'. He read it over to himself three times and then began to break it down into units to memorise. It fell into two parts, and without much hesitation he voiced the first of these:

> *Ah, love, let us be true*
> *To one another! for the world, which seems*
> *To lie before us like a land of dreams,*
> *So various, so beautiful, so new,*

Hath really neither joy, nor love, nor light,
Nor certitude, nor peace, nor help for pain;

The 'nors' produced a curious but familiar punctuation which made the whole thing easy to commit to memory. The next three lines gave him a little more difficulty, and he had to repeat them several times inside his head before they were mastered:

And we are here as on a darkling plain
Swept with confused alarms of struggle and flight,
Where ignorant armies clash by night.

He put all the lines together and spoke them inaudibly, just by moving his lips. The result was a delicious feeling of fear: even though he did not quite know what or where the darkling plain was to be found, it struck a chord of perfect truth with him. After some moments of reverence, he put the book down on the settee and went into the sitting-room where his sister was watching 'Rawhide' on the television. He sat beside her and became quickly absorbed by the western series.

The programme ran into another which he watched without interest. Becoming at last fidgety, he decided to go back out to the street and wait for supporters coming home from the match. He was keen to know the score. The street was very dimly lit by a lamp on the opposite side to his house. He crossed over to the light, and then continued walking slowly to the junction of Shaftesbury Square and the Donegall Road. There were not many people about. The oily odours from the recently-opened

Wimpy Bar were mixing with those of beer and sawdust coming from Mosie Hunter's pub. He crossed to the other side of Bradbury Place and stood for what seemed a long time looking in the window of a toyshop which had a yellow film on its surface and made the objects inside difficult to perceive. It was during his effort at window-gazing that he became conscious of the noise of people surging forward, rather similar to that made by the stampeding herds that he had seen in cowboy pictures.

The rumbling noise grew louder until the first wave of supporters broke on Shaftesbury Square, soon to be followed by the sea of red-white-and-blue which washed all in front of it. Hugh instinctively pulled back into the shop doorway and took up a position where he could watch the crowd from a distance. Even though he wanted to know the score, he was hesitant about approaching this tri-coloured human sea which was rolling forward with such boisterousness. He could hear bursts of laughter, snatches of sentences, parts of words that meant that the Blues had obviously won and that this mass was moved along by the infectious desire to relive the intense moments of the match. The sea surged onwards in one homogenous body.

Hugh watched, fascinated. Buses passed carefully by, packed with supporters partly hanging out of the windows, their ragged scarves flapping triumphantly backwards in the wind. After about fifteen minutes, the noise abated and the crowd began to tail off into little pockets straggling along the pavements. Hugh crossed back over to the Donegall Road and then began following stragglers down towards Great Victoria Street. The pavement was extremely wide here and he deliberately walked slowly so as to be overtaken. When one solitary supporter reached his level, Hugh turned to him and asked the score of the match.

"Two—one for the Blues," came a gruff, but proud reply. Hugh then asked who scored.

"Hamilton gat them both," came the same gruff sounds, and the man was about to increase his gait when Hugh again held him back with a question:

"Good match, was it?" The man looked at him with a grin.

"Fuckin' brilliant, son," he replied, spitting enthusiastically on the dark pavement and starting to walk faster. Hugh watched his back as the man moved with rapid jerking movements across the Square to the top of Bedford Street. Hugh was almost certain that, as the man went to turn into that street, he quickly removed his scarf.

He was not sure now whether to turn back and retrace his steps or go round the block via Albion Street. Since he was certainly closer to the latter, he continued on his way. He passed the various seedy shop fronts until he came to the church on the corner. As he was running his hand along the thickly painted railings which protected the front of the church, he saw Red, Oscar and Smiley step out of the gloom of a doorway on the opposite side of the street. Red was not the first to recognise him, but he was the first to speak.

"Whada 'bout ya, Hughey boy? Long time no see," came the genuinely warm greeting from him. Hugh was not really sure how to relate to Red, who was four years older. He could not decide whether or not he even liked him. His real name was Cal

142

Ross, but everyone called him Red because of his mop of unruly ginger hair. Rumour had it that he had been given the name because his father—whom he had never seen—was a GI who had come to Belfast from California. Cal was the scorched and abbreviated result of Irish-American dreams.

Hugh crossed Albion Street to talk a while with the others. They stood on the corner in the light of a butcher's shop and he could see that they had obviously been drinking. The three had never been interested in football and it had not even registered with them that there had just been a match at Windsor Park. Hugh told them that the Blues had won and that it had been a good game, from which they mistakenly concluded that he had been at the match. As it pleased him, he did not contradict this notion. Smiley made an almost inaudible grunt about the "Whites—Fenian bastards," but he was of no significance within the group, and nobody paid any attention to what he said.

Red had never been 'bad', even though he had often been in trouble with the police. He was the natural leader of the boys in the street, being older than most and very solidly built. He also had that touch of madness which meant that, when he was attacked, he lost all notion of when or where he was, and consequently fought with any opponent without consideration for his person. He would rarely start a fight, but once involved, would battle until destruction. These were his main credentials.

Dr Esler's surgery was the third door down from Albion Street and was the first house which kept a 'garden', surrounded by a four-foot wall at the front. In fact, the garden had been replaced by a series of concrete flags put down because the doctor chose to live elsewhere, and it was cheaper, and above all wiser, to maintain the front of his surgery in this way. The four boys went and sat upon the side wall with their backs to Great Victoria Street. From their slow and broken conversation, Hugh could detect a growing animosity to him which came from the fact that he had drifted away from the others who had become more closely bound by their daily appetite for intrigue and survival. He was about to head for home when a bus stopped in the middle of Shaftesbury Square.

Oscar's keen eye was quick to spot a white scarf round the neck of an adolescent who had alighted from the bus. The stranger stopped to look around him and gain his bearings—he had obviously got off the bus too early.

"There's a fuckin' Whites supporter!" said Oscar under his breath, as if he might be overheard. Ostensibly, there was no reaction from the boys. They sat immobile on the wall, Oscar, Smiley and Red deliberately not looking in the direction of the stranger who, having realised that he was on foreign turf, began to walk briskly towards them in the direction that the bus had just taken.

"What the fuck's *he* doin' here?" asked Smiley with exaggerated vindictiveness.

Red nodded for the two boys to get off the wall and start moving towards the entrance to Dr Esler's. Hugh suddenly began perspiring, and he flushed cold as he became aware of the wall which he was resolutely clinging to. He looked at Red, but the latter only confirmed what he had come to suspect.

"He shudn't be here," was the conclusive verdict that Red pronounced. There was no good in pleading that the youngster had obviously lost his way: it was an accepted fact that the penalty to pay for being in the wrong territory was a heavy one. Besides that, there was nothing to say, the boy was from the other side.

Oscar and Smiley stood on the pavement pretending to be engaged in conversation. When the boy passed the entrance to the surgery, Red jumped discreetly off the wall and moved sprightly until he was just behind him. The boy was about to move out of the way of Oscar and Smiley when Red's fist came crashing into the back of his head. As he began to fall forward, Smiley booted him viciously between the legs. Hugh followed the movement of his body which seemed to rise slowly in the air, but immediately Oscar jumped on him and pulled him to the ground. Hugh climbed down and moved to the other side of the wall where boots were flying into the prostrate body of the other youngster who had pulled his hands over his head. Red thought that he had wanted to hold on to his football scarf and quickly reached to wrench it from the cowering and bleeding form which curled foetus-like on the pavement.

"Don't come back here ya Fenian bastard!" shouted Smiley, and he lunged once more with his boot into the almost inert body which rolled over so that the boy's gaping mouth opened on to the night as if appealing for help. But no sound came forth. His eyes opened wide and made contact with Hugh who stood paralysed above him.

After one or two more half-hearted kicks, Red had had enough. He motioned to the others to leave off. There was no intention to kill, just to injure, to teach a lesson. He wasn't even sure that Whites supporters were 'Fenians', but so what? He was out of his territory and nobody should leave their own tribe. Hugh turned his back on the prostrate figure and followed the others into Albion Street, Red clutching the Distillery scarf like a trophy. But the trophy was evidently something which was disreputable to carry, for he held it at arm's length like an oily rag, and looked at it in disgust. When they got to the entry at the back of Kensington Street, he quickly discarded it into the darkness.

On reaching the bottom of Kensington Street, they stopped briefly. Red looked inquisitively at Hugh:

"Are ya comin' with 's?" he asked. Hugh shook his head, and said lamely that he had to finish some homework for the next day. Smiley laughed, shaking his head as if he had been expecting that answer, and together the three continued walking along Albion Street in the direction of Oscar's house. Hugh started off for home, but after about a dozen steps he turned round and walked back to the corner from where he watched the others until they disappeared from sight. He then walked slowly back to the church corner, wondering all the time if he was doing the right thing, and looking back over his shoulder to make sure the others were not watching him. He felt safe enough, since the shadow of the church hid him from view.

Looking down Great Victoria Street, Hugh could see a man bending over the outstretched body of the boy. Hugh wanted to get closer, to find out if he was going to be alright, but at the same time he was afraid. "I should have helped him," he said to himself, reproachfully. But even in the middle of his self-accusation he knew that it would have been impossible. The others would have turned on him even more viciously. There is nothing worse than a traitor.

Hugh approached the back of the man who was now kneeling over the boy. He looked over his shoulder at the tumescent face which seemed to be bleeding from several places. One eye was completely closed. He had fair hair which was short-cropped, but because of the disfigured face it was impossible to tell what age he was. From his clothes and tennis shoes, Hugh concluded that they must be about the same age.

"Is he alright?" he asked the man.

"Some bastards give 'im a kickin', so they did but there's a wee woman over there who's ringing for an ambulance." With one hand the man supported the boy's head and with the other he stroked his bloodied hair affectionately. The latter's body began to shake quietly as he silently wept.

"Ya'll be alright, son," said the man, as he went on stroking the fair hair.

An ambulance was soon on the spot and the boy was quickly gathered up and placed on a stretcher. As they carried him to the back of the vehicle, Hugh walked with them. At one point the boy looked up at him, staring fixedly with his one-seeing eye. Hugh's eyes were trying to say that he was sorry, but no words came from him. When he was safely in the back of the ambulance, the driver turned to Hugh:

"Is he a friend o' yours?" he asked half-expectantly.

"No," came the monosyllabic reply.

"Do ya know 'im at all?"

"No," Hugh answered, shaking his head.

"Did ya see what happened to 'im?" came the final question.

"No," he said sorrowfully, and he stepped back to let them close the doors. Before he could say anything else, the man who had been attending the fair-haired boy added:

"He came after me, so he cudn't 'a seen anything, for all I saw was a bunch o' young fellas headin' up Albion Street." Hugh breathed a sigh of relief.

As the ambulance sped off, Hugh said "Goodbye," to the man, and started walking home. He walked quite fast, as he was sure the police would soon arrive. When he got back to the street, he rested for some time against the window ledge of his house. He felt as if he wanted to vomit. He had not hurt anyone and he had not helped anyone. He had denied all knowledge of the event, but that was not the lie which pained him most. He was ridden by a deep sense of disgust, both for his 'friends' and for himself. The picture of the boy's tumescent face was lodged in his mind. He realised that he would have to erase it, if only momentarily. As he sat looking back on the evening, he remembered that the Blues had won the match two-one. This brought a faint smile and an ironic grunt from his lips. He decided to go into the house. He still had the last verse of 'Dover Beach' to commit to memory.

Touched

It was difficult to say what exactly was magical about the late spring afternoon: the sky was ordinarily blue with just a few puffy clouds; the sun breaking mildly on the back of Hugh's head as he walked across from the bus stop to the entrance to Barnett's Park. To the lad, it felt wonderful to be alive, but he could not say exactly why. Not that he needed to examine his feelings too closely. He was never depressed or gloomy. Getting up in the morning was like emerging from a chrysalis into a world awaiting his discovery. If, on top of that, his natural expectancy was matched by favourable meteorological conditions, his day took on this indefinably magical quality.

When he got to the park gates, he stopped and then heaved himself up onto the highest bar, in the shade of the canopy of trees. He was to meet Deirdre here. He looked around at the shaded and subtle array of green land and leaf which stretched backwards and forwards in a monotonous riot of monochromatic but subtle variation. He plucked a shiny leaf from the tree above his head and began rubbing its thick greenness between his finger and thumb. He flicked through a running list of tree-names in order to try to give a name to the leaf. But nature had remained something remote to him. It had taken him some time to realise that concrete and tarmac were not in fact the precursors of earth and grass; that it was indeed the latter which were the natural components of man's habitat. The leaf in his hand remained unidentified, which only moderately disturbed him as he was sufficiently content with his resolution that the tree it belonged to was an evergreen—which it was not. He continued to caress the leaf delicately between finger and thumb and then began tearing it along the veins, breaking it into little sharp pieces. He put several of the pieces to his nose. *That's how green smells,* he said to himself. Slowly raising his head, he identified in the distance the outline of Deirdre's approaching figure. Broken pieces of green fell through his long fingers as he became absorbed in her approach.

"Oh God!" he said audibly, as she came nearer. She must not have had time to change out of her school uniform for he could clearly distinguish her green blazer, white blouse, and green skirt. Why did she look so pathetic in her school uniform? Her legs were too thin and they were exposed almost cruelly by the short, green skirt. There was something very fragile and vulnerable about her legs that, when he looked at her, reminded him of a new-born deer struggling to maintain itself in an upright position. He watched her attentively as she now approached the park. His heart swelled.

Deirdre Morrigan was seventeen. Her hair was Irish, black-Irish, thick and waved and flicked with curls at the ends. One of the things he enjoyed most was to lie beneath her and raise the black masses above him, draw the deep strands out to heavy points and then let them crash down upon his face so that he could no longer see and was almost suffocated by the weight of her hair. She had freckles, a multitude of tiny reddish-brown blotches which dappled her cheeks and nose, but were limited above by the bar of her black Irish eyebrows, and below by the whitening skin which centred finally on the fullness of her purple-red lips. Her lips were not only full, but deep, the upper one arched in open and innocent invitation.

When she saw that he was looking at her, she accelerated her step until she stood on the opposite side of the road waiting for a black Austin to rush past. Hugh looked at her long, thin legs, following up the whiteness from the tops of her white school-socks to her thighs which fascinated him, but which, at the same time, he wanted to throw his jacket over. Her thighs were both naive and obscene, simultaneously full of attraction and repulsion, and always disturbing. He admitted to himself that he longed to touch them. Perhaps today he would. His blood seemed to thicken in his veins.

When she had crossed the Malone Road and was almost upon him, her lips pouted a long "Hello," and then widened into a smile that radiated warmth into him. They touched and kissed and he buried his face in her perfumed hair. When he had disentangled himself, he looked at her all flushed. He put his hands inside the sleeves of her blazer and gently stroked her forearms which were covered in small, fine hairs that tingled under his touch. A little smile stretched the corners of her mouth, and Hugh fancied that she was about to say something teasing, something playful which underlined her girlishness. He usually liked this, for a while.

"What?" he said to her coaxingly. But she did not reply. Instead, she bent forward and rubbed the fullness of her arched lips softly along the curve of his neck. It was a reverent movement which released his tension, and for which he was thankful.

Deirdre raised her head, then gently took his hand and they began to amble idly into the park, dodging dapples of sun that formed a Japanese pattern on the pathway in front of them. A wind suddenly waved the grass and half-turned the trees around them, causing the lighted pathway to blotch and merge and then reform again in a continual kaleidoscopic sway which contained them in its game of silhouettes.

"How long had you been waiting?" she asked, in an effort to make conversation.

"'Bout quarter of an hour," he replied, knocking forward a stone which came conveniently to foot.

"You're not angry with me, are you?"

"No, of course not, why should I be?"

"No reason … it's just that you look a bit angry. Maybe it's just me, though." Then after a short pause she added, "I suppose you took the afternoon off again?" She said this without aggression or resentment. They were both in their lower sixth year which meant that A-levels had begun to loom over the horizon. Although she was concerned about his recurrent missing of classes, she was nevertheless proud that he could do so and still get good results. It was part of her admiration for him.

"No, as a matter of fact I took the whole day off … I didn't get out of bed until half-ten. But it didn't really matter anyway as I only had biology and chemistry today." But Deirdre was correct to notice a tone of vexation which had been latent in his voice.

Much to the dismay of his science teachers, by the awkward and unforgiving age of seventeen, Hugh's sensibility had led him light years away from biology and chemistry. He no longer even made an effort to understand what was going on in class and refused to participate in any practical experiments, preferring to sit those periods out in a semi-daze until something he considered more worthy of his attention came along. He thought science was so mundane that it became an absurdity, leaving it impossible for him to appreciate the obvious seriousness of his science teachers. Secretly he hoped that they were just pretending to be involved with what they were doing, for no one he respected could possibly take Bunsen burners and test tubes seriously. He felt that missing a chemistry class was like missing an episode of 'Coronation Street', for you could inevitably pick up the thread the following week, or even month. But what vexed him presently was the unarticulated realisation that he had made the wrong choices for his A-levels, and that he was going to have to see his mistake right through to its conclusion. The only subject which comforted him in his examination years was literature.

When they reached a cast-iron bench, they sat down and stared at the shadowy gravel path at their feet. Deirdre believed that something was troubling him and she believed even more strongly that she knew exactly what it was. But she was adamant that she was not going to be the one to broach the subject. If anything, she would do her best to avoid it, and in the end relegate it to the realm of nebulous and unresolved life-mysteries.

Without premeditation, Hugh suddenly lifted his right hand and placed it on the girl's cheek which he began to strum with his thumb in an appeasing manner. She was surprised at this spontaneous gesture and moved her head to one side to capture his hand between cheek and shoulder. The position made her look coy. Hugh bent forward and kissed her. He had not meant to do that. Her lips, so open, so soft, became locked on to his so that he felt momentarily that he had fallen into a trap. The feeling made him recoil away from her and take his distance. She did not understand, but felt vaguely insulted, and quickly brought her head back to an upright position. He became moody, with a look of suffering in his eyes which she readily recognised. So, they would have it out yet again …

Hugh was both vexed and confused. His former irritation was now translating into his obsession. What was wrong with his head? He longed for her, but in this very longing his body contracted, something gripped his chest and cut short the breath which should have brought them closer together. He looked at the ground and then again at the whiteness of her thigh. And he resented her.

"Deirdre, we can't go on like this. You must tell me the truth, and don't say again that you can't tell—you must know."

"But why do you go on about it? I don't understand ... why it is so important to you?" Her tone suggested that she honestly could not understand why they had to go over the subject time and time again, it was just poison to them. He felt her tone was not perfectly ingenuous, but he could not answer her question. He had no answer. He didn't even understand the obsession himself. Something to do with poorly-conceived notions of purity and innocence. But it seemed to him that she did not need an answer, because she knew, perhaps even more than he did himself, why it was important. Her stubborn but half-hearted opposition to him told him that she knew.

"Tell me *exactly* what happened." His voice was cold, but his hands were becoming moist and sticky; he did not really want to hear what she was going to say.

"But I told you," she paused to collect herself then went on, "I was tipsy because we had been drinking cider all evening ... he was completely drunk ... we were dancing with everybody else and then we went along the beach ... the next thing I knew we were lying on the sand and he was touching me ... but I don't know whether or not he came inside me ..." She broke off and began sobbing.

He was oblivious to her suffering. Each word had burned into him so that he could neither hear nor see anything that was going on outside his own existence, he was aware of nothing outside his own pain. How could she say those words? She whose skin is so white and so innocent … how could she? What a filthy betrayal! *And she doesn't know whether or not she's a virgin! That's a good 'un!* His mind was running circles around him in leaps and bounds. His blood was in such a swim that it made him feel dizzy. *Why does it matter to me? Why?*

In the midst of her sobbing, Deirdre put her hands on his head and pulled him into her breasts. She kissed the back of his bowed head many times and covered him with her hair. The effect was soothing. Bit by bit, his blood came to a halt and he sat completely still with his head bowed on the cushion of her breasts, and the world cut off by the forest of her hair. He became restored to himself, and after a moment's perfect stillness, he lifted his head to emerge from the shield of her hair. He saw the grass and the trees in a crisp, fine light, and it was like seeing them for the first time—as if he had just been born again.

He looked into her eyes smudged with mascara. "I love you … I know that … you know that … but sometimes it just isn't enough, I don't know why …" For the present moment it was more than enough. He clutched her hair and kissed her quietly. The touch of her healed him, made him feel miraculously strong. He looked beyond her head to the fields which, perhaps for the first time, he felt part of, belonging to. *No, I mustn't think about it anymore … it's only destroying everything … and I mustn't punish her again … I must make it let go of me.* He wanted to protect Deirdre, not to hurt her. Where did this desire to destroy her come from? All that he knew was that, each time he had it in his head, he hated her. He loathed her and wanted to smash her and leave her like petals strewn upon the ground. This feeling would inevitably be followed by the desire to soothe her, the need to pick up the torn petals and reconstitute the flower of her. Each time he would resolve that she would not be abused again.

"Let's walk a little bit," he said aloud.

Deirdre had never been abused. If anything had passed between herself and that other boy on the beach, then she had willed it as much, if not more, than he had. Hugh wanted to see her as a victim when in fact her urge for life was so much more positive. Her instincts were too healthy for her to be a victim.

They walked down the gravelled path towards the White House, with their heads together, pausing for a moment to touch, then kiss, and then walk on. For Hugh, the afternoon opened up again and something magical flowed through them and the world they walked in. A new relation was established between himself and the trees, himself and the fields, the sky and the air itself. He felt part of the swirl of light and shadow and coloured oneness, the centre of it all.

They cut across fields and down the hill towards the river where they picked up the towpath which still followed the river for miles and miles. When he was younger, Hugh used to come often to this place for there were locks where you could get spricks and even eels. He had come once with his father to fish for trout. He remembered that day vividly, it was one of the few times he had ever done anything with his father. He could see the rounded figure of the man on the bank with his fishing rod. When he thought of his father he always saw him from a distance, unlike his mother who was always close to him sharing a relationship that he would qualify as being almost sightless. On that day, Hugh was a few feet above his father, sitting on the bank, observing him. They never talked very much. Most of the time the father would talk to himself, quietly. Hugh was quickly bored with fishing. He remembered having spent most of that day staring into the dark water stirring slowly below. There was a fish beside him in a plastic bag. He could smell the fish again as he walked along the path looking at the slimy mud of the river bank. He remembered the strange, dead eye of the fish. His father had said that it was dead, but every now and then it would flip its tail up and frighten the life out of him. He was unable to touch it, even through the plastic bag, and the trout ended up being given to the neighbour's cat when they got back home. But what a struggle it had put up! Torn from the water, it had flipped and wriggled in all sorts of contortions that broke the sunlight of the afternoon into colourful bits and pieces. And then it was dead, or almost. Hugh smiled as he thought of himself being frightened by the fish-flips. Deirdre asked his what he was smiling at.

"Nothing … I was just thinking about one day I went fishing a little bit further round the towpath there."

"I didn't know you liked fishing," she said.

"I don't!" he smiled again.

They walked on for some time, Hugh usually lost in the depth of the dark-flowing water; Deirdre usually lost in Hugh, in his silence which seemed to swallow her up in a deep envelope that surrounded her. She enjoyed his silence, it seemed to give her strength. It was his words that frightened her. The river meandered slowly forward, swaying stretched green fibres in the gentle waft of its motion. Further on, to the left, a channel broke away from the rest and the water there was pulled into a brisker pace which was made audible by a little fall on to pebbles and shingle. The sun caught the broken, forced tumble and shot out crazy spikes of light which were accompanied by shallow metallic noises and a deep gurgle like someone rinsing out a bowl. Sometimes the water of the river was sheened brilliant in the distance and sometimes split up into a myriad of winking eyes as the wind hit it at different points. But the main flow moved on resolutely, powerful in its lurid and fascinating darkness.

They walked on slowly, almost at the same pace as the river which must have communicated its slowness to them. Deirdre suddenly had had enough. She decided that they should move away from the river and the incomprehensible influence it had on them—especially on Hugh, who seemed to be leaving her behind as he moved deeper and deeper into silence. So she tugged at him with her will, acting against the current of the water, pulling him in the direction of an open field. He followed her rhythm.

"We'll walk through the big field and then back up the hill of the White House towards the flower-beds," she smiled at him and he obediently pressed his cheek against the side of her head.

"Do you love me?" she asked.

"Yes," yes, of course he did, but he hated saying it.

When they reached the hill again, they began struggling upwards, leaving the water behind, below. The sun beat down fully on the backs of their heads and they became hot and sweaty under its influence and the uphill effort. They saw a thick-set oak standing solidly in the middle of their path and they began to move more quickly towards it. When they reached it, they plumped down thankfully under its sinewy branches, the great entanglement of its shadowy weightiness blocking out the light and heat of the sun.

From where they sat, they had a view over the river and the lower hill opposite which ran down to the Giant's Ring on the right. There were two yew trees to the left, and just beyond them, two toy-like, motionless figures seated on the wall of the stone bridge. Deirdre and Hugh looked down upon them as from a watchtower. Wrapped as they were in the shade, they felt they could see without being seen. Since they were still hot, they decided to take off their shoes and socks and run their feet bare through the grass which was moist and cool. Then they began to play with each other. Deirdre put her feet on his chest and skilfully pulled open his shirt sufficiently to slip one foot on to his breast. She explored as far as possible without putting too much strain on the remaining buttons of his shirt. He took her other foot and bit her playfully on the ankle. She responded by withdrawing both, and then holding one in mid-air before him which she used to make wide circles just in front of his nose. The circles got smaller and smaller as if she was trying to hypnotise him. He made a snapping movement as if wanting to bite her again, but she was too fast for him, and quickly folded her legs below her and sat in an upright position. She sat challenging him, daring him to move.

"I feel like hitting you," he said.

"You just try!"

Which he did; he sprang at her and carried her backwards with his weight, but she would not surrender. She resisted with surprising energy as he tried to pin her arms to the grass. He knew that he was much stronger than the girl, but he did not want to be brutal, nor to hurt her. So when she pushed upwards again he let himself roll with the movement so that he brought her on top of him. He was happy in this position because he felt he could control her without hurting her. In fact they were both happy with the situation. They simultaneously decided upon a truce which was marked by her letting her lips drop on to his. They kissed frantically, both aware that their playfulness had inevitably been destined to end here, even, that this had been the unacknowledged objective of their play.

Deirdre wriggled on top of him until she made herself comfortable. It was the first time that they had ever been in that position, and even though the danger was diminished by her being on top, they nevertheless felt the excitement running through them. Hugh had his hands fully on her behind, which was also new for them as he had never dared go further than touch more than her breasts. They explored each other, each finger-advance into new territory. They became more and more intense. Deirdre began to writhe on top of him, her hands turning, exploring, pushing and pulling at his clothing, becoming more reckless in her movements. Then, by contrast, she gently slithered her hand down on to his trousers, and further down until she could feel his penis under her fingertips. The event was so unexpected that it made him almost convulse with ecstasy and he made a violent movement upwards with his limbs. The movement surprised Deirdre who immediately rolled off him until they both lay breathless and looking up at the dark canopy of the tree which weighed like a lid on top of them.

Even though she was still out of breath, Deirdre made an attempt to break through the silence where only their breathing was clearly audible. "I … I knew that would happen … knew it would … I told you about it before … we shouldn't lie down together …" Her tone was one of self-reproach, but for some reason it struck him as being false. But he did not care that she was insincerely rebuking herself for her boldness. After all, he had been the willing object of her audacity.

She went on talking, but he was no longer listening. Instead, he floated off into the world around, letting himself be carried on the various currents of the afternoon: the leaves, the clouds, the fleeting sunlight, all turning and swirling and whisking him along so that he was almost light-headed. The world swished and flowed and he was the centre of it all.

As his breathing returned to normal and his body stopped heaving, things began to slow up and to fall back into a pattern which he was more used to. He became conscious of a thin, metallic sound which he reluctantly identified as Deirdre's voice. The words were now punctuated by tears. He turned his head to look at her. Again she was not convincing. *Why does she have to do this?* he asked himself. He suspected that she was putting on a show for him, one that he did not want, that she did not need to put on. He was also ashamed at feeling a distance between them, a distance created by her need to pretend, and by

162

his seeing through that pretence. But he would not be callous with her. How could he be, when all he wanted was for her to touch him again? He said the words over and over again in his head: *Touch me, touch me, touch me,* and he almost hoped that she could hear them. However, Deirdre was occupied with her outward display of guilt and recrimination. She lay with her hands on her face, ostensibly locked up in herself, but secretly opening her arms to him.

When he spoke, she was relieved: "Don't be silly," he said encouragingly, "I loved it … honestly I did … it was really superb," and he stroked her face gently, catching a tear with his finger which he put to his lips. Kindly, he let her play her part, and when she was convinced that things had gone on long enough, she sat upright and kissed him.

The afternoon was turning into early evening and the dropping sun began to enflame the small clouds. It was time to go home, the dampness of the earth was growing cold. In silence, they put on their socks and shoes and rose to their feet. They stood together in an embrace for some time. He looked down at the river which no longer had surface, only depth, now much darker than before. The toy-like figures beyond the yew trees had disappeared. The sun beyond the hill opposite was throwing up coloured spears and lances through the clouds, renting them into streaks of reds and golds. He felt as if he was standing for the first time at the centre of something glorious, something a million light years away from the greys and blacks of the streets of Sandy Row. He was thankful to be part of it. Turning to Deirdre he said, "Yes, I love you." It was a statement of his plenitude, brought about by the majestic setting surrounding them, forced up and out of him almost like sap.

They walked towards the flower beds where a man was picking up tools and placing them in a wheelbarrow. He was aware of their approach. Every now and then he would raise his red and healthy face, as if he was waiting for the right moment to say something. When they were near enough, he saluted them in a warm, friendly voice. "Won't be long nigh before we're inta summer," he said, waiting for an answer.

"Today will do me," said Hugh, looking into the gardener's cheeky eyes.

"Aye, but there's nathin' like summer. It does me good ta hear youngsters singin' and talkin' and runnin' about—as long as they don't touch the flar beds, mind ya," and he made a clucking sound as he winked to them. They decided that it was getting too late to spend anytime looking at the flowers, and so they bade the gardener goodbye, to which he replied with an affectionate "All the best."

They walked in step towards the park gates, along the path which had become gloomy now that there was no longer sunlight on the grass or shafting the trees. Hugh felt that things would no longer be the same between them, that a stronger connection had now been established. He had not really wanted it, but it was real enough. He was confident that they would take this even further within the not-too-distant future.

As he walked along musing on these thoughts, he became aware of a curious wetness in his trousers. He pushed his free hand discreetly into his trousers. *Christ!* he said to himself, *I've*

164

come! He was not unhappy in his discomfort. On the contrary, it made him feel stronger and gave him a peculiar satisfaction which caused him to smile like a sphinx. Even in the semi-obscurity she could distinguish his smile which, although puzzling, reassured her.

Soon they had reached the wide arch of the main gates and advanced into the road beyond where traffic was starting to build up. They crossed to the bus stop and stood holding each other with his back to the traffic like a shield.

"What will you say to your parents for being late?" he asked her with obvious concern.

"Don't know … but I'll think of something on the way back." She had about a ten-minute walk along the Malone Road before reaching home. "And you?"

"Nobody ever asks me anything," his reply was both reassuring and disappointing.

"What time will I see you tomorrow?" He knew she had no classes the next day, which was not his case. He thought for a minute, looking fixedly at her short, green skirt and then replied,"I'll come to your house at about two, okay?"

"Great!" They pecked and hugged each other until her eye caught his bus coming round the bend.

"There's your bus, you'd better go," she said hurriedly, reaching out her lips to him. He kissed her a short, hectic kiss and then jumped on board just in time. The bus moved off before they had time to say anything else, and the girl quickly receded into the growing obscurity and distance. He paid his fare to the conductor and went upstairs.

The harsh, artificial lights of the bus made the outside look even darker. After a few minutes on the road, it stopped at traffic lights, and a gap in the buildings meant that Hugh caught sight of a startling, dark-flamed redness in the sky to the west. It formed a sort of cavern, which was roofed by some thicker cloud which had now gathered. As he looked into the blaze, he felt rich, in possession of a multitude of precious fires. He became aware once more of the wetness in his trousers. As the bus moved off, and he gazed for a last time into the sunset, a smile again came to his lips.

"I've come!" he said to himself, happily.

Gentle into that Good Night

Conor's mother had died some two months previously. He had looked after her almost single-handedly for about eighteen years—ever since she had become confined to a wheelchair. He had made the decision not to get married in order to devote himself entirely to his mother. The decision had been relatively easy to take since he was attached to no one else, and no woman seemed capable of generating in him the feelings he had decided were necessary for any marriage to be successful. So he had moved from one girlfriend to another, never getting deeply involved, and always returning to wait on his invalid mother who clung to him much more strongly than she did to the sturdy chair which transported her frail body. He was now in his mid-forties, alone after her death, and at the end of a road which seemed to have come back to a point he had known some twenty years previously. He was filled with frustration and loss, and the feeling that he had come full circle made his present emptiness seem all the more unbearable.

Religion had held him together for a long time. He was not much of a churchgoer. Neither did he see any reflection of his religious sentiments in the people who lived near him, most of whom were staunch Protestants and went to church at least once a week. He cared nothing for the outward manifestations of religion, but nevertheless, he had a profound conviction that there was a life after this one, and that his decision to care for his mother was undoubtedly sanctioned from above. In fact, when all the accounts were drawn up, this was one of the few things that would figure on the positive side, and just might help him gain access to the next world. But somehow, inexplicably, his deep-seated conviction volatilised when his mother's spirit left her body. Nothing remained for him to get a firm hold of, and he was now completely at a loss.

The evening was alighting upon Kensington Street. The neon tubes perched on their concrete posts began to pale the air with a dun-coloured light which, all of a sudden, seemed to intensify the descending gloom. Conor regretted the passing of the old gas lamps. He liked the popping and wheezing noise they had made—it struck a chord in him, and was peculiarly comforting. "I'm just oul-fashioned," he said to himself, as the pale fevered light intensified and shafted the room which gave on to the street. "I'm oul before ma time," he muttered sardonically.

Conor let himself drop heavily into one of the armchairs drawn up to the fireplace which was prepared with tightly twisted coils of newspaper, sticks and anthracite—the only fuel that could be burned in these days of smokeless coal. The ready fire looked as if it was waiting for someone to come home from work. Conor stared at the perfectly rounded black nuggets and decided that he had no intention of lighting the fire. Not tonight, and probably not tomorrow night either.

He lay his head back and gently lapsed into reverie. The room faded as he began to fall through the years until he found himself under the old lamp post, which was sputtering and coughing and dimly lighting the face of the girl from the Donegall Pass that he shared a desk with at school. Dana's hair was jet black, but it appeared streaked with blue under the gas light.

"Hi can you do the sums when I can't?" he asked her smilingly. Dana didn't answer. Her eyes lit up cheekily and her lips revealed the naked whiteness of her perfectly shaped teeth. "You have lovely teeth Dana," he said appreciatively.

Conor moved slightly in his chair, still unconscious of the room and the yellowing light spilling in through the window. "And her hair, God she had beautiful hair … I would have loved to have touched her hair." He moved his neck slowly until his head found a more comfortable hollow, and then settled down again into his childhood.

Dana was James's girlfriend. James was a good friend of his. He lived just across the street and they used to call for each other to go to school each morning. But he was so argumentative! Conor and he had so many fights because James always wanted to have the last word. Even after he had fought and was beaten, he would still utter the last word under his breath as he was walking away.

"Aggravatin' gat!" said Conor, as he rolled his head over.

But he liked James. As youngsters they had always played together. Early adolescence had brought them very close, only to be separated later by James's going out with Dana.

"I think she fancied me, though." Conor remembered how she had put her arm around him when the three were walking home from a party. He had become quite embarrassed, and was afraid that James might suspect something. But he had never responded.

"I never tried to get off with her," he told himself vaguely, "but God, did she have beautiful hair!"

James had married Dana and they had left Kensington Street to live somewhere near the border. He hadn't heard from them in years, and hadn't tried to contact them. In his semi-consciousness, Conor was suddenly aware once more of a chilling sense of loss.

"Where are you James?" The words were almost audible and the movement of his lips stirred him out of his reverie and pushed him back into the enlightened darkness of the tiny room.

Night had fallen. His eyes adjusted to the shafted gloom and the objects in the room steadily took shape before him. He had not sat in the dark for a long time. Since his mother died he had become almost frightened of the dark. He smiled bitterly at the thought and determined immediately to take a stand against the night. He would have to be brave.

The room was cold. He crossed his legs and pulled them against the armchair. He felt goose pimples on his arms and so he thrust his hands between his thighs to warm them. He shivered. The shivering strangely made him feel that there was someone in the room, and his first reaction was to move to put the light on. But he quickly checked his impulse and told himself that it was just nonsense, that he was tired and needed rest. He turned his head sideways into the enveloping cushion of the armchair and tried to bury his nose deep into the worn velvet. The material felt warm, and as he breathed into it, he became increasingly aware of an odour which was unmistakably that of his mother. He used to lift her into this chair in the evenings. Now, from the depths of its threadless material came her perfume of faded rose petals. The perfume carried him again through the years to the picture of a young boy walking sleepily by his mother's side. They had been visiting friends and it was very late. Once outside the friend's house, his mother opened her coat and enveloped him in its warmth. As they walked along, his head bobbed on the movement of her hip, and his senses swam in the sweet-scented odours that were distantly mingled with the bitter smell of nicked cigarettes rising from her pinafore pocket. Conor held on tightly and blindly to her waist as they rode the footpaths to their house. On arrival, he was cruelly ejected from the warmth of the coat as his mother fiddled with the key to open the door, but he was then quickly scooped out of the night again and projected into the warmth of home.

Conor turned his head from the velvet upholstery and gazed once more into the sombre grate. He knew that he would have to shake himself, that there was no way he could go on like this. But it was just that there was nothing stronger to pull at him, to pull him out of the past. He stood at a crossroads where all the roads led backwards to the same point, and this realisation filled him with nausea.

As he sat in silent dejection, there came the sound of several voices coarsely mingling and slowly increasing in volume until Conor was sure that they came from just outside his front door. For some reason, they had come to a halt outside this door, but they did not knock on it. He waited expectantly and listened attentively. He clearly distinguished three voices, which were holding a muddled sort of colloquy. They were easily distinguishable because of relatively long pauses between what seemed to be broken bits of sentences left hanging in the air and then tediously picked up again. The fragments were sometimes incoherent, but adamantly punctuated by swear words uttered with particular violence.

"… catch the fucker … 'e thinks 'e can do me outa a tenner … catch 'im 'n' knock 's fuckin' balls in …" The speaker seemed to be having difficulty breathing. Conor wondered who he was and who he could be talking about, but this curiosity was overshadowed by embarrassment. On both sides of his house lived old ladies whom he thought would be very upset by the swearing—if they were listening to what was going on outside, as they probably were.

"'E's a cunt … nat the first time th' bastard's tried to do us … we'll catch 'im …" another voice had taken up from the first. A third added his suggestion as to what they should do with the culprit once they had caught up with him. The speech of all three came together into an offensive slur where soon only the swear words were clearly audible.

"They must be drunk," said Conor to himself, as he moved closer to the window to see the sources of what he considered to be unacceptable filth. One person was leaning on the shoulder of another who had his back to Conor, but whose other shoulder was obviously propping both men up against the wall. The third was out of his range of vision, but must have his back against the front door. Conor recognised the only face that was given to his view without obstruction as being that of a young buck from the top of Wesley Street. All three were certainly young, probably in their late teens or early twenties. They were part of the new generation which had begun to take things into their own hands, and controlled various shadowy enterprises which had become the bread and butter of the neighbourhood's now embittered and battle-hardened out-of-work.

Conor listened uneasily to their laboured exchanges which were becoming more intense, and consequently louder. He recognised a rubbing sound of leather and metal against the wood of the front door and he discerned what he took to be someone's supporting foot sliding down the wooden panels of his door. He had had enough, and made up his mind that it was time they cleared off. He went into the small hallway, which gave on to the street, and stood suspended on his side of the door, behind someone whose breathing seemed to be erratic and frantically driven by the search for oxygen. He hesitated for a few moments more, in the hope that the three would suddenly decide to take themselves off without any intervention. But he was disappointed, and it was with a certain reluctance that he took the snib off the door and began opening it. Despite the fact that he performed the latter operation rather tentatively, the person with his back to the door nevertheless fell backwards—almost in slow motion it seemed to Conor—until he found himself flat on his back. The other two scrutinised Conor as if they were trying to distinguish some recognisable feature in his appearance.

"Listen lads, could you not go a bit further up the street … I can't even hear the TV." Conor spoke in a coaxing tone which was tinged with a friendly attempt at humour.

"Who th' fuck are you?" came from the young buck from Wesley Street. Conor looked straight at him and was intrigued by his eyes which were so wide-pupilled that there was hardly any colour to them. He wanted to say that he meant no harm, and that there were old people living nearby, but he was overcome by a great sense of fatigue and futility. He wanted them to go, but knew instinctively that they would not go now until they had made an issue out of it. Because the young man on the ground was toiling unsuccessfully to get into a sitting position, Conor decided to give him a hand. He bent down and motioned to put his forearms under the arms of the struggling body. At the same moment, the boot of the young man opposite came crashing into the side of his head. Conor fell backwards against the flimsy inner door which quickly gave way under his weight, and soon found himself spread out ignominiously in his own sitting room.

As Conor lay face down on the thick carpet with his ear on fire and a scorched sensation burning across the side of his head, the two lads on their feet tugged energetically at their struggling accomplice until they managed to prop him upright. This accomplished, the Wesley Street buck advanced into the sitting room.

"I ast ya a fuckin' question, are ya deaf?" and again his boot came crashing into Conor's prostrate body, which curled under the impact. The other two came stumbling forward and, having caught the smell of blood, they began to kick the curled up figure which contracted convulsively under each drunken blow. One of them fell over as his foot slid off the top of Conor's ribs, and the heaviness of his clumsy body smashed into the back of the armchair which he overturned in his fall, and broke.

The others helped him again to his feet, and all three stood gasping for air, intoxicated and breathless after the delivery of blows whose destructive energy had somehow brought them to their senses. They looked at the inert supine body, the face already swollen and disfigured, the red leaking on to the thick carpet. They realised that it was time for them to clear off. Before making their way out of the room, they checked the kitchen to verify that no one else was present, and one of them—without the knowledge of his friends—picked up Conor's wallet which was sitting on the mantelpiece.

They were gone as inexplicably as they had come. Conor was vaguely aware that he was alone again in his house. He could feel no pain in the total immobile numbness which had taken over what was his body. Even, there was a strange element of pleasure in the complete insensitivity which bathed him thickly in a glow of warmness. But somewhere, in the far-off corner of his consciousness, he was aware that something was leaving him, that there was a flow of life which was inevitably draining away from him. And he was not unhappy about the situation.

As he felt his life softly seeping out of him, Conor distinguished voices caressing him, and especially the mild chantings of an aged female voice: *God help us! God help us! God love ya son!* He saw his mother standing over him. She could stand and move, she was no longer paralysed. She bent forward and smiled at him and he smiled back lovingly.

"Dear God what's he smilin' at?" asked old Mrs Neville from two doors up. She put her hand under his head and was taken aback by the hideous sight of the blood trickling from the corner of Conor's perfect smile.

"Get an ambulance … for God's sake somebody get an ambulance!"

One of the neighbour's sons, Hugh McDonnell, had already run to Mosie Hunter's public house to call for an ambulance. He had been the first on the scene, and had immediately connected the three staggering figures he had seen only minutes before going up the street, with the lain-out figure he now distinguished thanks to the yellow light which flooded into the room from the street. He had not seen their faces, but had a good idea who the attackers were.

Hugh stood in the doorway watching as the bent-over figure of Mrs Neville wiped the distorted face clean of its bloodied stains. He had just finished his A-levels and was about the same age as Conor's attackers. If his suspicions proved right, these were the boys he had grown up with, the boys with whom he had shared all the experiences—the pains and pleasures—of childhood and early adolescence. Going to the grammar school had wedged difference between them and had taken Hugh into a new sphere of contact, whilst leaving them to turn in the predictable cycles of violence and destruction. He was overcome by a feeling of revulsion as he looked at Conor's punished and trampled body, at the life that they had tried to stamp out. When the ambulance came, and Conor was being carried out of his house, Hugh too, noticed the smile which unmistakably pushed back the inflated cheeks which would otherwise have swallowed his mouth. No one present could guess what on earth he was smiling at.

Conor remained in hospital for several days. His life seemed to be out of danger, but he was not making any progress. Nothing seemed to be able to bring him back into this world and he would spend his conscious time simply lying back and gazing fixedly at the ceiling. The police left him alone for the first couple of days and then tried to interview him, but he gave no sign that he recognised the sense of their questioning. After reassurances by the neighbours that they would look after him, the doctors decided to let him go home.

The neighbours put up a bed in the downstairs room, partly for convenience, but mainly because they felt instinctively that the proximity to the street was a tightening of the bond which linked Conor to his life. But Conor did not respond to the street or to any external stimulus. Visitors came and went without the slightest indication that he was on the road to recovery. Indeed, some saw in his fixed stare the condemnation of their own life, which made them want to get away as fast as they could. When he shut his eyes and slept, there was often intense activity with a frantic to-and-fro movement which suggested that there was a fierce struggle going on within. But his conscious life gave not a suspicion of this.

After about a week at home, Conor was visited by Hugh McDonnell. The lad had told the police that he had seen three people walking up Kensington Street shortly before he had discovered Conor on the floor, but he did not tell them that he thought he had recognised them. He waited in the hope that Conor, once conscious, would identify his attackers. But this had not happened. So he sat beside the bed and waited until he was alone with the patient. At first, he spoke only about the start of the summer and the good weather which had just come to Belfast, and Conor seemed to be responding, however minimally, to his presence. Hugh was encouraged to go on.

"It was Oscar McAsheen that gave you the kickin', wasn't it?" Conor turned his head faintly to one side until he could see into the eyes of the teenager. He looked at him at length, and with an immutable softness which made Hugh feel ill at ease. Then he closed his eyes and his life began again to run ever so quietly, but definitively, away from him.

After some time spent watching the suspension of Conor's breathing, Hugh went to inform the neighbours, who were quick to occupy the house. When they were satisfied that the boy's conclusion was correct, they began making preparations for the formalities which were to be accomplished. Mrs Neville said bitterly that Conor "had been kicked to death," but Hugh could not accept this. He left the others to their bitterness and sorrow and went down to the bottom of the street where he turned the corner and stood for some time with his back to the wall. People were moving about busily in the fading light of the early evening and the pubs were already beginning to fill up. About fifty yards away he could distinguish a familiar silhouette which was coming in his direction. He felt frightened. The figure must have come out of the entry which ran between the backs of the houses of Kensington Street and the shops of Shaftesbury Square. It was Oscar McAsheen. He was staggering in ragged movements of deliberate slowness. When he reached the bottom of Kensington Street, he saw Hugh on the corner, and began staggering drunkenly towards him. Oscar had no reason to think that Hugh might suspect him of being implicated in the kicking, as nothing had filtered through from police inquiries.

Hugh did not know how to react to the approaching figure. He felt alien and sick. When Oscar had come right up to him, Hugh looked into the other's dilated eyes. Oscar had great difficulty in keeping his eyes fixed on Hugh, for they pulled upwards as if he was about to collapse. He unexpectedly threw his arms around Hugh.

"Bin ages since a saw ya … ages … don't pay any attention t' me … bin on th' oul hearts." He pulled Hugh closely into his neck and hugged him clumsily. When he managed to free himself a little from the violent affection of Oscar's grasp, Hugh saw that the other lad was sobbing quietly.

"Yar right ta get outa here … thar's nathin' here for ya … get away from here … don't turn out like me." Oscar was now crying profusely in the despair of his own circumstances and the genuine desire to absolve his one-time friend of any guilt that he may feel about having deserted his former friends and all that accompanied them. Oscar squeezed his shoulders with a desperate grip that penetrated deep into Hugh's body. Then he turned and left, and went staggering on up Kensington Street, wiping the tears streaming down his cheeks with the edge of the tattered and blackened cuff of his shirt.

Hugh fell back against the wall. He felt sad beyond tears. Images of Conor's bloated and deformed face came to him, but the picture which stilled his mind was that of the smile on the deadened body they had carried out on the stretcher. He pulled himself away from the wall and turned into Kensington Street where he could just glimpse the fading, tottering figure of Oscar McAsheen who had reached the Donegall Road. Hugh walked slowly towards home, oppressed by the nearness of the darkened bricks, sickened by the promiscuity of the large blank windows of the houses which seemed to be looking incredulously into one another. He had to get away. He passed Conor's house on the opposite side of the street. It, like the rest, felt alien to him.

They didn't kick him to death, was the thought that struck him as he looked resentfully along the row of identical houses huddled together in the narrowness of their complicity.

Toilet Blues

June 1972. The height of the Troubles. On a late Wednesday evening, Hugh sat in his mother's chair beside the swept-out hearth. The room was silent and he could hear a mouse scraping against the wallpaper as it scrambled up the crumbling wall. He felt tired. It was summer and his A-levels were thankfully well behind him. His mother had left for England. Her nerves were bad. She had gone to get the bus in Shaftesbury Square but had forgotten her purse. Lucky that. She went back to her house to get her money when a small bomb went off. It was in the litter bin at the bus stop. Not a big explosion, just enough to break a woman's heart.

It was the last straw. She left Belfast within the week. Left Hugh with his father to tie ends up and see to the furniture, the remnants of which would eventually find their way to Lancashire. He didn't mind her going. He felt he understood. They were very close, and he would certainly have encouraged her to leave, except that she never gave him the opportunity to do so. Now he sat brooding on the empty grate. He couldn't be bothered enough to bang the wall with his fist to send the unsuspecting mouse to the floor.

Hugh's da was on vigilante duty this evening. Hugh was spared that because of his 'education'. The street had a lot of respect for education. Vigilante duty for Mr McDonnell meant walking with his neighbour to the top of Sandy Row, left along the Donegall Road, round Shaftesbury Square and back up Albion Street to the Row, with a big wooden stick. A cyclical walk that lasted about four hours. It was a time of machine guns and Armalite rifles but his da had a big wooden stick. Hugh smiled into the grate: *Barney Rubble and Fred Flintstone against the Enemies of the Empire* ... he said to himself.

His da had made the tea, as usual. This was not because his mother had left, his father often cooked for the three of them, well, ever since she had had her accident. Hugh rose and went to the scullery were the dishes were piled up in the sink. He began washing up. Despite the clatter of dishes, he suddenly became aware of an abundance of noise from outside. He paused and looked up through the skylight. Either there was an exceptional number of shooting stars this evening or the trails he could see were tracer bullets streaming across the sky. At that moment, he heard the hall doors burst open and quickly turned round to look through the window behind him. He saw the dishevelled figure of his father rush into the centre of the room. Hugh put down the plate he was holding and went into the sitting room.

"What's wrong?" Unlike all his friends, Hugh never called his father 'da'—except in jest—because his father was English. He avoided calling him anything, except in mind conversations when he used 'da'.

Looking at his son, the father pushed his thick black hair backwards with both hands. The stick, which was leaning against his thigh, he then took and propped up against the wall beside the settee. "That won't be much use tonight," he said prophetically.

"Why, what's wrong?"

"They say the Taigs are comin' up the Pass." His father looked at him fixedly, staring into his eyes, which produced an unusual exchange between them. Hugh felt a bit panicky. He wasn't really afraid of the situation, simply of the intensity of the exchange. His father recognised the fear immediately. "It's alright, son, they'll not get us here."

"I'll finish the dishes and make a cup of tea."

"Aye, thanks."

His father began tidying things up, hanging up his coat, arranging bits and pieces in the room. A tremendous bang was heard outside. He moved quickly to the outside door and secured it. Then he did the same to the door which gave on to the sitting room. During this time, Hugh went on with the dishes, conscious of bullets screaming overhead. No one would really kill them. They had never done any harm.

Then he remembered that time when his friend Geordie had taken him to that dance in the markets area … they had only been there five minutes when three or four boys jumped on him and started thumping and kicking him until he was thankfully pushed out into the street with his nose and face running with blood. His mother had just bought him this new light suit which was now covered in red. He hadn't done anything—he was just there. He hadn't been afraid, well, hadn't had time to be afraid. But maybe tonight they should be afraid.

The tea was ready. They both drank silently looking into the grate. The noise outside was getting louder and louder. There was a screeching sound which split open the pings and stammers of bullet fire.

"I think son we might be better spending a wee bit o' time in the toilet." His father was a sensible man. It was true that if the Taigs ever managed to gunfight their way up the Pass, then Kensington Street was the first street on their route after Shaftesbury Square. It made sense not to stay in the house. They could be torched. This was a time of torching, after all, the Prods had torched rows of houses near the Shankill, on some streets you had people who lived where they weren't wanted.

The toilet was a very sturdy edifice. Mr McDonnell had built it all with his own hands. He had been away in Gibraltar with the RAF when Hugh was just a child and had been called home urgently with the news that his wife had had an accident. He came home to find her in the Royal Victoria. She had decided to whitewash the back wall, which meant walking between flimsily-supported panes of glass. She was not a heavy woman but one false step meant that she ended up with seventy-two stitches in her legs. She was ripped and scarred and close to death. Mr McDonnell immediately decided to tear down the scullery and build a new, concrete roof and walls, keeping the toilet and coalhole separate at the back. This is where they would now find shelter for a while.

After moving through the scullery, they stood exposed to the evening sky. Hugh was already much taller than his father. But he felt awkward and propped his back against the wall of the coalhole. Neither of them even glanced at the toilet which was the only seat available. Mr McDonnell looked wistfully into the air, a small space which he had created in order to have access to the roof. The stutter of rifle fire made him draw instinctively closer to his son. In spite of being much taller, Hugh was aware of the presence of his father, his broad shoulders protectively shielding the teenager. When the firing increased to a indistinguishable uninterrupted cross-stammer, the boy lowered his head so that the sky was blocked out by the bulk of his father's dominant body.

For some time, the father talked about anything that was in any way reassuring: football, about which he knew nothing; boxing, about which he knew a lot. He had been a boxing champion in the RAF, the only testimony to this being his very thick earlobes. He had been small, compact, fast. He always said, you hit first and ask questions later, always much better to regret having hit someone than to regret not having hit him. A logic Hugh could understand but which remained alien to him. He had a lot of admiration for his father's pugnacious body but he did not share his philosophy. It was a costly discrepancy and a gulf between them which could never really be crossed.

The firing lightened for a moment and Hugh looked into his father's still-black, full, silky hair. His father's youthful manliness made him suddenly resentful.

"Why did you never take us to Gibraltar?" The question rang out like a shot in the comparative lull. His father moved slowly backwards.

"I tried to bring you all, son. I tried. Your ma didn't want to come. You know what it's like ... she had her cronies here ... she never wanted to leave Belfast. I had a house and everything ready in married quarters, but she wouldn't come. And then she fell through the roof."

Hugh looked at the concrete roof his father had put up and felt that there was truth in what he was saying. Yet, he was still not completely convinced, there was something that couldn't let him come over to his father's side.

"But there wasn't just Gibraltar ... you could have taken us to England."

"Aye, I could ... I had the offer of married quarters several times, but it was always the same old story ..."

The father sensed his son's resentment, a sort of nagging antagonism. But he wasn't willing to address it. There was nothing that he felt he had to justify, a man doesn't have to justify his choices to his children. Hugh would have his own choices to make. He had lived his life as fully as he could and regretted nothing. Regret was useless, not part of him. Difficulties he had always simply shrugged off. He had always been a loner; he found people easy to get on with but even easier to forget. As a married man and father he had ruled his home with an iron fist, or rather, a leather belt, which his children, with the exception of Hugh, had often felt. When he was away with the Air Force he lived as a single man, no cares or responsibilities, a man women liked. He felt his son should not resent him for this, after all, he would be a man too.

"You're a worrier son."

Hugh looked again into his father's small brown eyes which seemed to contract. He waited for him to go on.

"Son, I'll tell you something … and you listen to me. You see my hair? I've still got all my hair and it's still jet black—you know why? I'll tell you why … I've never worried about a thing in my life, so I haven't, not a thing, and that's the God's truth."

"We're not the same."

"Oh, I know that son! You're just like my brother Sid. He was a worrier. Smart fella. He died skinny as a rake, baldy, a bundle of nerves. I tell you son, it's not worth it. You've only got one life, be good to it."

Hugh was momentarily distracted by louder and louder bursts of machine-gun fire. He thought of the irony of the situation—men cutting each other to pieces outside his door and here was his father telling him not to worry about anything! He smiled to himself. The father caught the smile in the lit-up night.

"That's right son, better to laugh about things! You know, your problem is that you're too smart for your own good. Tell you the truth, I don't know where you got your brains from—it wasn't from your ma, that's for sure! There was Sid … aye, he was hell of a smart fella … always reading books and wouldn't talk to you … he wouldn't talk to anybody, kept himself to himself, wasn't interested in other people's business. He wouldn't spend Christmas, either! Tight git, he was!"

Mr McDonnell wandered off into childhood reminiscences which were barely audible because of the noise around them. The night overhead was becoming enflamed in destructive confrontation. Hugh looked down at the coal spilled around his feet. His father thought that he was brooding again.

"Don't take things too seriously, son. In another few days we'll be away from here and you'll be starting university in England. You'll have a great time!"

Hugh looked up at him. He knew he was in for some more advice. He was right.

"Remember son, it's the same with women … don't get bogged down. Love them and leave them son, that's the best bit of advice I can give you … love them and leave them."

Hugh thought over these manly words as he stared at the figure who had given him life. How far had he followed his own advice?—this man who had got married when he was twenty and had had four children without even thinking about it. How many women had this man loved and left? When and where? Maybe one day he would come across a half-brother or sister no one knew about! Wouldn't surprise him.

It took a few moments for Mr McDonnell to realise that his son might be putting two and two together and just might be thinking about things he shouldn't be thinking about—that it was not at all his business to be thinking about!

"Well son, you'll have your own life to live … all I can say is that you should make the most of it. You're a long time dead."

Hugh smiled again. A silence stood between them. They both looked awkwardly upwards and began following the traces of bullets criss-crossing the sky in fine streaks pulled across the dancing light and dark. Hugh didn't want to resent his father. Life couldn't have been that simple for him, born an Englishman, living in Belfast. He had always been and would always be an outsider, a stranger, different from the others. In the street he was known as Mr McDonnell, the Englishman, and respected for his gentlemanly and gallant ways. The years had changed his accent until it was no longer Midlands but not yet Belfast. In between two islands. When he would return to England he would sometimes get into a fight because of someone calling him 'Paddy'. He was essentially on his own, a loner. Not really a man for children, they could never make up the focus of his life, more of a by-product than an objective. He had a different philosophy of life—a different 'outlook', as he referred to it—and would always remain his own man, a free agent.

The couple stood for a long time together in the cooling night air, exchanging every now and then brief utterances of banalities, snippets of life. Despite several uncomfortable and even antagonistic moments, Hugh still felt an inevitable closeness to this man who would willingly stand between him and the world, sheltering him from danger, if he could.

After several hours spent in the toilet, the noise around them abated somewhat and receded into the normal stuttering of sporadic gunfire. Mr McDonnell decided that there was no longer much of a risk and ushered his son back into the house. After tidying the scullery a bit, Hugh went up to his bedroom. The window of the latter gave on to the backs of the houses from Wesley Street. He kept the light off and undressed quickly in the dark. As he stood for a moment looking out of his bedroom window he could hear his father's heavy footsteps coming up the stairs.

"Goodnight, son," came softly and with a certain hesitancy from just outside his door.

"Goodnight … da." His father went into his own bedroom and Hugh listened as he climbed into the creaky bed.

Hugh was happy that very soon he would leave Sandy Row. He was happy too, on thinking over the hours he had just spent standing with his father in the shelter of the toilet, that he had finally made the acquaintance of someone who had, up to this point, essentially been a benevolent stranger to him.